A Prefect's Uncle

by

P. G. Wodehouse

[1]

TERM BEGINS

Marriott walked into the senior day-room, and, finding no one there, hurled his portmanteau down on the table with a bang. The noise brought William into the room. William was attached to Leicester's House, Beckford College, as a mixture of butler and bootboy. He carried a pail of water in his hand. He had been engaged in cleaning up the House against the conclusion of the summer holidays, of which this was the last evening, by the simple process of transferring all dust, dirt, and other foreign substances from the floor to his own person.

"Ullo, Mr Marriott,' he said.

'Hullo, William,' said Marriott. 'How are you? Still jogging along? That's a mercy. I say, look here, I want a quiet word in season with the authorities. They must have known I was coming back this evening. Of course they did. Why, they specially wrote and asked me. Well, where's the red carpet? Where's the awning? Where's the brass band that ought to have met me at the station? Where's anything? I tell you what it is, William, my old companion, there's a bad time coming for the Headmaster if he doesn't mind what he's doing. He must learn that life is stern and life is earnest, William. Has Gethryn come back yet?'

William, who had been gasping throughout this harangue, for the intellectual pressure of Marriott's conversation (of which there was always plenty) was generally too much for him, caught thankfully at the last remark as being the only intelligible one uttered up to present date, and made answer—

'Mr Gethryn 'e's gorn out on to the field, Mr Marriott. 'E come 'arf an hour ago.'

'Oh! Right. Thanks. Goodbye, William. Give my respects to the cook, and mind you don't work too hard. Think what it would be if you developed heart disease. Awful! You mustn't do it, William.'

Marriott vanished, and William, slightly dazed, went about his professional duties once more. Marriott walked out into the grounds in search of Gethryn. Gethryn was the head of Leicester's this term, *vice* Reynolds departed, and Marriott, who was second man up, shared a study with him. Leicester's had not a good name at Beckford, in spite of the fact that it was generally in the running for the cricket and football cups. The fact of the matter was that, with the exception of Gethryn, Marriott, a boy named Reece, who kept wicket for the School Eleven, and perhaps two others, Leicester's seniors were not a good lot. To the School in general, who gauged a fellow's character principally by his abilities in the cricket and football fields, it seemed a very desirable thing to be in Leicester's. They had been runners-up for the House football cup that year, and this term might easily see the cricket cup fall to them. Amongst the few, however, it was known that the House was passing through an unpleasant stage in its career. A House is either good or bad. It is seldom that it can combine the advantages of both systems. Leicester's was bad.

This was due partly to a succession of bad Head-prefects, and partly to Leicester himself, who was well-meaning but weak. His spirit was willing, but his will was not spirited. When things went on that ought not to have gone on, he generally managed to avoid seeing them, and the things continued to go on. Altogether, unless Gethryn's rule should act as a tonic, Leicester's was in a bad way.

The Powers that Be, however, were relying on Gethryn to effect some improvement. He was in the Sixth, the First Fifteen, and the First Eleven. Also a backbone was included in his anatomy, and if he made up his mind to a thing, that thing generally happened.

The Rev. James Beckett, the Headmaster of Beckford, had formed a very fair estimate of Gethryn's capabilities, and at the moment when Marriott was drawing the field for the missing one, that worthy was sitting in the Headmaster's study with a cup in his right hand and a muffin (half-eaten) in his left, drinking in tea and wisdom simultaneously. The Head was doing most of the talking. He had led up to the subject skilfully, and, once reached, he did not leave it. The text of his discourse was the degeneracy of Leicester's.

'Now, you know, Gethryn—another muffin? Help yourself. You know, Reynolds—well, he was a capital boy in his way, capital, and I'm sure we shall all miss him very much—*but* he was not a good head of a House. He was weak. Much too weak. Too easy-going. You must avoid that, Gethryn. Reynolds....' And much more in the same vein. Gethryn left the room half an hour later full of muffins and good resolutions. He met Marriott at the fives-courts.

'Where have you been to?' asked Marriott. 'I've been looking for you all over the shop.'

'I and my friend the Headmaster,' said Gethryn, 'have been having a quiet pot of tea between us.'

'Really? Was he affable?'

'Distinctly affable.'

'You know,' said Marriott confidentially, 'he asked me in, but I told him it wasn't good enough. I said that if he would consent to make his tea with water that wasn't two degrees below lukewarm, and bring on his muffins cooked instead of raw, and supply some butter to eat with them, I might look him up now and then. Otherwise it couldn't be done at the price. But what did he want you for, really?'

'He was ragging me about the House. Quite right, too. You know, there's no doubt about it, Leicester's does want bucking up.'

'We're going to get the cricket cup,' said Marriott, for the defence.

'We may. If it wasn't for the Houses in between. School House and Jephson's especially. And anyhow, that's not what I meant. The games are all right. It's—'

'The moral *je-ne-sais-quoi*, so to speak,' said Marriott. 'That'll be all right. Wait till we get at 'em. What I want you to turn your great brain to now is this letter.'

He produced a letter from his pocket. 'Don't you bar chaps who show you their letters?' he said. 'This was written by an aunt of mine. I don't want to inflict the whole lot on you. Just look at line four. You see what she says: "A boy is coming to Mr Leicester's House this term, whom I particularly wish you to befriend. He is the son of a great friend of a friend of mine, and is a nice, bright little fellow, very jolly and full of spirits."'

'That means,' interpolated Gethryn grimly, 'that he is up to the eyes in pure, undiluted cheek, and will want kicking after every meal and before retiring to rest. Go on.'

'His name is—'

'Well?'

'That's the point. At this point the manuscript becomes absolutely illegible. I have conjectured Percy for the first name. It may be Richard, but I'll plunge on Percy. It's the surname that stumps me. Personally, I think it's MacCow, though I trust it isn't, for the kid's sake. I showed the letter to my brother, the one who's at Oxford. He swore it was Watson, but, on being pressed, hedged with Sandys. You may as well contribute your little bit. What do you make of it?'

Gethryn scrutinized the document with care.

'She begins with a D. You can see that.'

'Well?'

'Next letter a or u. I see. Of course. It's Duncan.'

'Think so?' said Marriott doubtfully. 'Well, let's go and ask the matron if she knows anything about him.'

'Miss Jones,' he said, when they had reached the House, 'have you on your list of new boys a sportsman of the name of MacCow or Watson? I am also prepared to accept Sandys or Duncan. The Christian name is either Richard or Percy. There, that gives you a fairly wide field to choose from.'

'There's a P. V. Wilson on the list,' said the matron, after an inspection of that document.

'That must be the man,' said Marriott. 'Thanks very much. I suppose he hasn't arrived yet?'

'No, not yet. You two are the only ones so far.'

'Oh! Well, I suppose I shall have to see him when he does come. I'll come down for him later on.'

They strolled out on to the field again.

'In *re* the proposed bucking-up of the House,' said Marriott, 'it'll be rather a big job.'

'Rather. I should think so. We ought to have a most fearfully sporting time. It's got to be done. The Old Man talked to me like several fathers.'

'What did he say?'

'Oh, heaps of things.'

'I know. Did he mention amongst other things that Reynolds was the worst idiot on the face of this so-called world?'

'Something of the sort.'

'So I should think. The late Reynolds was a perfect specimen of the gelatine-backboned worm. That's not my own, but it's the only description of him that really suits. Monk and Danvers and the mob in general used to do what they liked with him. Talking of Monk, when you embark on your tour of moral agitation, I should advise you to start with him.'

'Yes. And Danvers. There isn't much to choose between them. It's a pity they're both such good bats. When you see a chap putting them through the slips like Monk does, you can't help thinking there must be something in him.'

'So there is,' said Marriott, 'and it's all bad. I bar the man. He's slimy. It's the only word for him. And he uses scent by the gallon. Thank goodness this is his last term.'

'Is it really? I never heard that.'

'Yes. He and Danvers are both leaving. Monk's going to Heidelberg to study German, and Danvers is going into his pater's business in the City. I got that from Waterford.'

'Waterford is another beast,' said Gethryn thoughtfully. 'I suppose he's not leaving by any chance?'

'Not that I know of. But he'll be nothing without Monk and Danvers.

He's simply a sort of bottle-washer to the firm. When they go he'll

collapse. Let's be strolling towards the House now, shall we? Hullo!

Our only Reece! Hullo, Reece!'

'Hullo!' said the new arrival. Reece was a weird, silent individual, whom everybody in the School knew up to a certain point, but very few beyond that point. His manner was exactly the same when talking to the smallest fag as when addressing the Headmaster. He rather gave one the impression that he was thinking of something a fortnight ahead, or trying to solve a chess problem without the aid of the board. In appearance he was on the short side, and thin. He was in the Sixth, and a conscientious worker. Indeed, he was only saved from being considered a swot, to use the vernacular, by the fact that from childhood's earliest hour he had been in the habit of keeping wicket like an angel. To a good wicket-keeper much may be forgiven.

He handed Gethryn an envelope.

'Letter, Bishop,' he said. Gethryn was commonly known as the Bishop, owing to a certain sermon preached in the College chapel some five years before, in aid of the Church Missionary Society, in which the preacher had alluded at frequent intervals to another Gethryn, a bishop, who, it appeared, had a see, and did much excellent work among the heathen at the back of beyond. Gethryn's friends and acquaintances, who had been alternating between 'Ginger'—Gethryn's hair being inclined to redness— and 'Sneg', a name which utterly baffles the philologist, had welcomed the new name warmly, and it had stuck ever since. And, after all, there are considerably worse names by which one might be called.

'What the dickens!' he said, as he finished reading the letter.

'Tell us the worst,' said Marriott. 'You must read it out now out of common decency, after rousing our expectations like that.'

'All right! It isn't private. It's from an aunt of mine.'

'Seems to be a perfect glut of aunts,' said Marriott. 'What views has your representative got to air? Is *she* springing any jolly little fellow full of spirits on this happy community?'

'No, it's not that. It's only an uncle of mine who's coming down here. He's coming tomorrow, and I'm to meet him. The uncanny part of it is that I've never heard of him before in my life.'

'That reminds me of a story I heard—' began Reece slowly. Reece's observations were not frequent, but when they came, did so for the most part in anecdotal shape. Somebody was constantly doing something which reminded him of something he had heard somewhere from somebody. The unfortunate part of it was that he exuded these reminiscences at such a leisurely rate of speed that he was rarely known to succeed in finishing any of them. He resembled those serial stories which appear in papers destined at a moderate price to fill an obvious void, and which break off abruptly at the third chapter, owing to the premature decease of the said periodicals. On this occasion Marriott cut in with a few sage remarks on the subject of uncles as a class. 'Uncles,' he said, 'are tricky. You never know where you've got 'em. You think they're going to come out strong with a sovereign, and they make it a shilling without a blush. An uncle of mine once gave me a threepenny bit. If it hadn't been that I didn't wish to hurt his feelings, I should have flung it at his feet. Also I particularly wanted threepence at the moment. Is your uncle likely to do his duty, Bishop?'

'I tell you I don't know the man. Never heard of him. I thought I knew every uncle on the list, but I can't place this one. However, I suppose I shall have to meet him.'

'Rather,' said Marriott, as they went into the House; 'we should always strive to be kind, even to the very humblest. On the off chance, you know. The unknown may have struck it rich in sheep or something out in Australia. Most uncles come from Australia. Or he may be the boss of some trust, and wallowing in dollars. He may be anything. Let's go and brew, Bishop. Come on, Reece.'

'I don't mind watching you two chaps eat,' said Gethryn, 'but I can't join in myself. I have assimilated three pounds odd of the Headmagisterial muffins already this afternoon. Don't mind me, though.'

They went upstairs to Marriott's study, which was also Gethryn's. Two in a study was the rule at Beckford, though there were recluses who lived alone, and seemed to enjoy it.

When the festive board had ceased to groan, and the cake, which Marriott's mother had expected to last a fortnight, had been reduced to a mere wreck of its former self, the thought of his aunt's friend's friend's son returned to Marriott, and he went down to investigate, returning shortly afterwards unaccompanied, but evidently full of news.

'Well?' said Gethryn. 'Hasn't he come?'

'A little,' said Marriott, 'just a little. I went down to the fags' room, and when I opened the door I noticed a certain weird stillness in the atmosphere. There is usually a row going on that you could cut with a knife. I looked about. The room was apparently empty. Then I observed a quaint object on the horizon. Do you know one Skinner by any chance?'

'My dear chap!' said Gethryn. Skinner was a sort of juvenile Professor Moriarty, a Napoleon of crime. He reeked of crime. He revelled in his wicked deeds. If a Dormitory-prefect was kept awake at night by some diabolically ingenious contrivance for combining the minimum of risk with the maximum of noise, then it was Skinner who had engineered the thing. Again, did a master, playing nervously forward on a bad pitch at the nets to Gosling, the School fast bowler, receive the ball gaspingly in the small ribs, and look round to see whose was that raucous laugh which had greeted the performance, he would observe a couple of yards away Skinner, deep in conversation with some friend of equally villainous aspect. In short, in a word, the only adequate word, he was Skinner.

'Well?' said Reece.

'Skinner,' proceeded Marriott, 'was seated in a chair, bleeding freely into a rather dirty pocket-handkerchief. His usual genial smile was hampered by a cut lip, and his right eye was blacked in the most graceful and pleasing manner. I made tender inquiries, but could get nothing from him except grunts. So I departed, and just outside the door I met young Lee, and got the facts out of him. It appears that P. V. Wilson, my aunt's friend's friend's son, entered the fags' room at four-fifteen. At four-fifteen-and-a-half, punctually, Skinner was observed to be trying to rag him. Apparently the great Percy has no sense of humour, for at four-seventeen he got tired of it, and hit Skinner crisply in the right eyeball, blacking the same as per illustration. The subsequent fight raged gorily for five minutes odd, and then Wilson, who seems to be a professional pugilist in disguise, landed what my informant describes as three corkers on his opponent's proboscis. Skinner's reply was to sit down heavily on the floor, and give him to understand that the fight was over, and that for the next day or two his face would be closed for alterations and repairs. Wilson thereupon harangued the company in well-chosen terms, tried to get Skinner to shake hands, but failed, and finally took the entire crew out to the shop, where they made pigs of themselves at his expense. I have spoken.'

'And that's the kid you've got to look after,' said Reece, after a pause.

'Yes,' said Marriott. 'What I maintain is that I require a kid built on those lines to look after me. But you ought to go down and see Skinner's eye sometime. It's a beautiful bit of work.'

[2]

INTRODUCES AN UNUSUAL UNCLE

On the following day, at nine o'clock, the term formally began. There is nothing of Black Monday about the first day of term at a public school. Black Monday is essentially a private school institution.

At Beckford the first day of every term was a half holiday. During the morning a feeble pretence of work was kept up, but after lunch the school was free, to do as it pleased and to go where it liked. The nets were put up for the first time, and the School professional emerged at last from his winter retirement with his, 'Coom *right* out to 'em, sir, right forward', which had helped so many Beckford cricketers to do their duty by the School in the field. There was one net for the elect, the remnants of last year's Eleven and the 'probables' for this season, and half a dozen more for lesser lights.

At the first net Norris was batting to the bowling of Gosling, a long, thin day boy, Gethryn, and the professional—as useful a trio as any school batsman could wish for. Norris was captain of the team this year, a sound, stylish bat, with a stroke after the manner of Tyldesley between cover and mid-off, which used to make Miles the professional almost weep with joy. But today he had evidently not quite got into form. Twice in successive balls Gosling knocked his leg stump out of the ground with yorkers, and the ball after that, Gethryn upset his middle with a beauty.

'Hat-trick, Norris,' shouted Gosling.

'Can't see 'em a bit today. Bowled, Bishop.'

A second teaser from Gethryn had almost got through his defence. The Bishop was undoubtedly a fine bowler. Without being quite so fast as Gosling, he nevertheless contrived to work up a very considerable speed when he wished to, and there was always something in every ball he bowled which made it necessary for the batsman to watch it all the way. In matches against other schools it was generally Gosling who took the wickets. The batsmen were bothered by his pace. But when the M.C.C. or the Incogniti came down, bringing seasoned county men who knew what fast bowling really was, and rather preferred it on the whole to slow, then Gethryn was called upon.

Most Beckfordians who did not play cricket on the first day of term went on the river. A few rode bicycles or strolled out into the country in couples, but the majority, amongst whom on this occasion was Marriott, sallied to the water and hired boats. Marriott was one of the six old cricket colours—the others were Norris, Gosling, Gethryn, Reece, and Pringle of the School House—who formed the foundation of this year's Eleven. He was not an ornamental bat, but stood quite alone in the matter of tall hitting. Twenty minutes of Marriott when in form would often completely alter the course of a match. He had been given his colours in the previous year for making exactly a hundred in sixty-one minutes against the Authentics when the rest of the team had contributed ninety-eight. The Authentics made a hundred and eighty-four, so that the School just won; and the story of how there were five men out in the deep for him, and how he put the slow bowler over their heads and over the ropes eight times in three overs, had passed into a school legend.

But today other things than cricket occupied his attention. He had run Wilson to earth, and was engaged in making his acquaintance, according to instructions received.

'Are you Wilson?' he asked. 'P.V. Wilson?'

Wilson confirmed the charge.

'My name's Marriott. Does that convey any significance to your young mind?'

'Oh, yes. My mater knows somebody who knows your aunt.'

'It is a true bill.'

'And she said you would look after me. I know you won't have time, of course.'

'I expect I shall have time to give you all the looking after you'll require. It won't be much, from all I've heard. Was all that true about you and young Skinner?'

Wilson grinned.

'I did have a bit of a row with a chap called Skinner,' he admitted.

'So Skinner seems to think,' said Marriott. 'What was it all about?'

'Oh, he made an ass of himself,' said Wilson vaguely.

Marriott nodded.

'He would. I know the man. I shouldn't think you'd have much trouble with Skinner in the future. By the way, I've got you for a fag this term. You don't have to do much in the summer. Just rot around, you know, and go to the shop for biscuits and things, that's all. And, within limits of course, you get the run of the study.'

'I see,' said Wilson gratefully. The prospect was pleasant.

'Oh yes, and it's your privilege to pipe-clay my cricket boots occasionally before First matches. You'll like that. Can you steer a boat?'

'I don't think so. I never tried.'

'It's easy enough. I'll tell you what to do. Anyhow, you probably won't steer any worse than I row, so let's go and get a boat out, and I'll try and think of a few more words of wisdom for your benefit.'

At the nets Norris had finished his innings, and Pringle was batting in his stead. Gethryn had given up his ball to Baynes, who bowled slow leg-breaks, and was the most probable of the probables above-mentioned. He went to where Norris was taking off his pads, and began to talk to him. Norris was the head of Jephson's House, and he and the Bishop were very good friends, in a casual sort of way. If they did not see one another for a couple of days, neither of them broke his heart. Whenever, on the other hand, they did meet, they were always glad, and always had plenty to talk about. Most school friendships are of that description.

'You were sending down some rather hot stuff,' said Norris, as Gethryn sat down beside him, and began to inspect Pringle's performance with a critical eye.

'I did feel rather fit,' said he. 'But I don't think half those that got you would have taken wickets in a match. You aren't in form yet.'

'I tell you what it is, Bishop,' said Norris, 'I believe I'm going to be a rank failure this season. Being captain does put one off.'

'Don't be an idiot, man. How can you possibly tell after one day's play at the nets?'

'I don't know. I feel so beastly anxious somehow. I feel as if I was personally responsible for every match lost. It was all right last year when John Brown was captain. Good old John! Do you remember his running you out in the Charchester match?'

'Don't,' said Gethryn pathetically. 'The only time I've ever felt as if

I really was going to make that century. By Jove, see that drive?

10

Pringle seems all right.'

'Yes, you know, he'll simply walk into his Blue when he goes up to the

Varsity. What do you think of Baynes?'

'Ought to be rather useful on his wicket. Jephson thinks he's good.'

Mr Jephson looked after the School cricket.

'Yes, I believe he rather fancies him,' said Norris. 'Says he ought to do some big things if we get any rain. Hullo, Pringle, are you coming out? You'd better go in, then, Bishop.'

'All right. Thanks. Oh, by Jove, though, I forgot. I can't. I've got to go down to the station to meet an uncle of mine.'

'What's he coming up today for? Why didn't he wait till we'd got a match of sorts on?'

'I don't know. The man's probably a lunatic. Anyhow, I shall have to go and meet him, and I shall just do it comfortably if I go and change now.'

'Oh! Right you are! Sammy, do you want a knock?'

Samuel Wilberforce Gosling, known to his friends and admirers as Sammy, replied that he did not. All he wanted now, he said, was a drink, or possibly two drinks, and a jolly good rest in the shade somewhere. Gosling was one of those rare individuals who cultivate bowling at the expense of batting, a habit the reverse of what usually obtains in schools.

Norris admitted the justice of his claims, and sent in a Second Eleven man, Baker, a member of his own House, in Pringle's place. Pringle and Gosling adjourned to the School shop for refreshment.

Gethryn walked with them as far as the gate which opened on to the road where most of the boarding Houses stood, and then branched off in the direction of Leicester's. To change into everyday costume took him a quarter of an hour, at the end of which period he left the House, and began to walk down the road in the direction of the station.

It was an hour's easy walking between Horton, the nearest station to Beckford, and the College. Gethryn, who was rather tired after his exertions at the nets, took it very easily, and when he arrived at his destination the church clock was striking four.

'Is the three-fifty-six in yet?' he asked of the solitary porter who ministered to the needs of the traveller at Horton station.

'Just a-coming in now, zur,' said the porter, adding, in a sort of inspired frenzy: "Orton! 'Orton stertion! 'Orton!' and ringing a bell with immense enthusiasm and vigour.

11

Gethryn strolled to the gate, where the station-master's son stood at the receipt of custom to collect the tickets. His uncle was to arrive by this train, and if he did so arrive, must of necessity pass this way before leaving the platform. The train panted in, pulled up, whistled, and puffed out again, leaving three people behind it. One of these was a woman of sixty (approximately), the second a small girl of ten, the third a young gentleman in a top hat and Etons, who carried a bag, and looked as if he had seen the hollowness of things, for his face wore a bored, supercilious look. His uncle had evidently not arrived, unless he had come disguised as an old woman, an act of which Gethryn refused to believe him capable.

He enquired as to the next train that was expected to arrive from London. The station-master's son was not sure, but would ask the porter, whose name it appeared was Johnny. Johnny gave the correct answer without an effort. 'Seven-thirty it was, sir, except on Saturdays, when it was eight o'clock.'

'Thanks,' said the Bishop. 'Dash the man, he might at least have wired.'

He registered a silent wish concerning the uncle who had brought him a long three miles out of his way with nothing to show at the end of it, and was just turning to leave the station, when the top-hatted small boy, who had been hovering round the group during the conversation, addressed winged words to him. These were the winged words—

'I say, are you looking for somebody?' The Bishop stared at him as a naturalist stares at a novel species of insect.

'Yes,' he said. 'Why?'

'Is your name Gethryn?'

This affair, thought the Bishop, was beginning to assume an uncanny aspect.

'How the dickens did you know that?' he said.

'Oh, then you are Gethryn? That's all right. I was told you were going to be here to meet this train. Glad to make your acquaintance. My name's Farnie. I'm your uncle, you know.'

'My what?' gurgled the Bishop.

'Your uncle. U-n, un; c-l-e—kul. Uncle. Fact, I assure you.'

[3]

THE UNCLE MAKES HIMSELF AT HOME

'But, dash it,' said Gethryn, when he had finished gasping, 'that must be rot!'

'Not a bit,' said the self-possessed youth. 'Your mater was my elder sister. You'll find it works out all right. Look here. A, the daughter of B and C, marries. No, look here. I was born when you were four. See?'

Then the demoralized Bishop remembered. He had heard of his juvenile uncle, but the tales had made little impression upon him. Till now they had not crossed one another's tracks.

'Oh, all right,' said he, 'I'll take your word for it. You seem to have been getting up the subject.'

'Yes. Thought you might want to know about it. I say, how far is it to

Beckford, and how do you get there?'

Up till now Gethryn had scarcely realized that his uncle was actually coming to the School for good. These words brought the fact home to him.

'Oh, Lord,' he said, 'are you coming to Beckford?'

The thought of having his footsteps perpetually dogged by an uncle four years younger than himself, and manifestly a youth with a fine taste in cheek, was not pleasant.

'Of course,' said his uncle. 'What did you think I was going to do?

Camp out on the platform?'

'What House are you in?'

'Leicester's.'

The worst had happened. The bitter cup was full, the iron neatly inserted in Gethryn's soul. In his most pessimistic moments he had never looked forward to the coming term so gloomily as he did now. His uncle noted his lack of enthusiasm, and attributed it to anxiety on behalf of himself.

'What's up?' he asked. 'Isn't Leicester's all right? Is Leicester a beast?'

'No. He's a perfectly decent sort of man. It's a good enough House. At least it will be this term. I was only thinking of something.'

'I see. Well, how do you get to the place?'

'Walk. It isn't far.'

'How far?'

'Three miles.'

'The porter said four.'

'It may be four. I never measured it.'

'Well, how the dickens do you think I'm going to walk four miles with luggage? I wish you wouldn't rot.'

And before Gethryn could quite realize that he, the head of Leicester's, the second-best bowler in the School, and the best centre three-quarter the School had had for four seasons, had been requested in a peremptory manner by a youth of fourteen, a mere kid, not to rot, the offender was talking to a cabman out of the reach of retaliation. Gethryn became more convinced every minute that this was no ordinary kid.

'This man says,' observed Farnie, returning to Gethryn, 'that he'll drive me up to the College for seven bob. As it's a short four miles, and I've only got two boxes, it seems to me that he's doing himself fairly well. What do you think?'

'Nobody ever gives more than four bob,' said Gethryn.

'I told you so,' said Farnie to the cabman. 'You are a bally swindler,' he added admiringly.

'Look 'ere,' began the cabman, in a pained voice.

'Oh, dry up,' said Farnie. 'Want a lift, Gethryn?'

The words were spoken not so much as from equal to equal as in a tone of airy patronage which made the Bishop's blood boil. But as he intended to instil a few words of wisdom into his uncle's mind, he did not refuse the offer.

The cabman, apparently accepting the situation as one of those slings and arrows of outrageous fortune which no man can hope to escape, settled down on the box, clicked up his horse, and drove on towards the College.

'What sort of a hole is Beckford?' asked Farnie, after the silence had lasted some time.

'I find it good enough personally,' said Gethryn. 'If you'd let us know earlier that you were coming, we'd have had the place done up a bit for you.'

This, of course, was feeble, distinctly feeble. But the Bishop was not feeling himself. The essay in sarcasm left the would-be victim entirely uncrushed. He should have shrunk and withered up, or at the least have blushed. But he did nothing of the sort. He merely smiled in his supercilious way, until the Bishop felt very much inclined to spring upon him and throw him out of the cab.

There was another pause.

'Farnie,' began Gethryn at last.

'Um?'

'Doesn't it strike you that for a kid like you you've got a good deal of edge on?' asked Gethryn.

14

Farnie effected a masterly counter-stroke. He pretended not to be able to hear. He was sorry, but would the Bishop mind repeating his remark.

'Eh? What?' he said. 'Very sorry, but this cab's making such a row. I say, cabby, why don't you sign the pledge, and save your money up to buy a new cab? Eh? Oh, sorry! I wasn't listening.' Now, inasmuch as the whole virtue of the 'wretched-little-kid-like-you' argument lies in the crisp despatch with which it is delivered, Gethryn began to find, on repeating his observation for the third time, that there was not quite so much in it as he had thought. He prudently elected to change his style of attack.

'It doesn't matter,' he said wearily, as Farnie opened his mouth to demand a fourth encore, 'it wasn't anything important. Now, look here, I just want to give you a few tips about what to do when you get to the Coll. To start with, you'll have to take off that white tie you've got on. Black and dark blue are the only sorts allowed here.'

'How about yours then?' Gethryn was wearing a somewhat sweet thing in brown and yellow.

'Mine happens to be a First Eleven tie.'

'Oh! Well, as a matter of fact, you know, I was going to take off my tie. I always do, especially at night. It's a sort of habit I've got into.'

'Not quite so much of your beastly cheek, please,' said Gethryn.

'Right-ho!' said Farnie cheerfully, and silence, broken only by the shrieking of the cab wheels, brooded once more over the cab. Then Gethryn, feeling that perhaps it would be a shame to jump too severely on a new boy on his first day at a large public school, began to think of something conciliatory to say. 'Look here,' he said, 'you'll get on all right at Beckford, I expect. You'll find Leicester's a fairly decent sort of House. Anyhow, you needn't be afraid you'll get bullied. There's none of that sort of thing at School nowadays.'

'Really?'

'Yes, and there's another thing I ought to warn you about. Have you brought much money with you?'

"Bout fourteen pounds, I fancy,' said Farnie carelessly.

'Fourteen *what*!' said the amazed Bishop. '*Pounds!*'

'Or sovereigns,' said Farnie. 'Each worth twenty shillings, you know.'

For a moment Gethryn's only feeling was one of unmixed envy. Previously he had considered himself passing rich on thirty shillings a term. He had heard legends, of course, of individuals who come to School bursting with bullion, but never before had he set eyes upon such an one. But after a time it began to dawn upon him that for a new boy at a public school, and especially at such a House as Leicester's had become under the rule of the late Reynolds and his predecessors, there might be such a thing as having too much money.

'How the deuce did you get all that?' he asked.

'My pater gave it me. He's absolutely cracked on the subject of pocket-money. Sometimes he doesn't give me a sou, and sometimes he'll give me whatever I ask for.'

'But you don't mean to say you had the cheek to ask for fourteen quid?'

'I asked for fifteen. Got it, too. I've spent a pound of it. I said I wanted to buy a bike. You can get a jolly good bike for five quid about, so you see I scoop ten pounds. What?'

This ingenious, if slightly unscrupulous, feat gave Gethryn an insight into his uncle's character which up till now he had lacked. He began to see that the moral advice with which he had primed himself would be out of place. Evidently this youth could take quite good care of himself on his own account. Still, even a budding Professor Moriarty would be none the worse for being warned against Gethryn's *bete noire*, Monk, so the Bishop proceeded to deliver that warning.

'Well,' he said, 'you seem to be able to look out for yourself all right, I must say. But there's one tip I really can give you. When you get to Leicester's, and a beast with a green complexion and an oily smile comes up and calls you "Old Cha-a-p", and wants you to swear eternal friendship, tell him it's not good enough. Squash him!'

'Thanks,' said Farnie. 'Who is this genial merchant?'

'Chap called Monk. You'll recognize him by the smell of scent. When you find the place smelling like an Eau-de-Cologne factory, you'll know Monk's somewhere near. Don't you have anything to do with him.'

'You seem to dislike the gentleman.'

'I bar the man. But that isn't why I'm giving you the tip to steer clear of him. There are dozens of chaps I bar who haven't an ounce of vice in them. And there are one or two chaps who have got tons. Monk's one of them. A fellow called Danvers is another. Also a beast of the name of Waterford. There are some others as well, but those are the worst of the lot. By the way, I forgot to ask, have you ever been to school before?'

16

'Yes,' said Farnie, in the dreamy voice of one who recalls memories
from the misty past, 'I was at Harrow before I came here, and at
Wellington before I went to Harrow, and at Clifton before I went to
Wellington.'

Gethryn gasped.

'Anywhere before you went to Clifton?' he enquired.

'Only private schools.'

The recollection of the platitudes which he had been delivering, under the impression that he was talking to an entirely raw beginner, made Gethryn feel slightly uncomfortable. What must this wanderer, who had seen men and cities, have thought of his harangue?

'Why did you leave Harrow?' asked he.

'Sacked,' was the laconic reply.

Have you ever, asks a modern philosopher, gone upstairs in the dark, and trodden on the last step when it wasn't there? That sensation and the one Gethryn felt at this unexpected revelation were identical. And the worst of it was that he felt the keenest desire to know why Harrow had seen fit to dispense with the presence of his uncle.

'Why?' he began. 'I mean,' he went on hurriedly, 'why did you leave
Wellington?'

'Sacked,' said Farnie again, with the monotonous persistence of a
Solomon Eagle.

Gethryn felt at this juncture much as the unfortunate gentleman in *Punch* must have felt, when, having finished a humorous story, the point of which turned upon squinting and red noses, he suddenly discovered that his host enjoyed both those peculiarities. He struggled manfully with his feelings for a time. Tact urged him to discontinue his investigations and talk about the weather. Curiosity insisted upon knowing further details. Just as the struggle was at its height, Farnie came unexpectedly to the rescue.

'It may interest you,' he said, 'to know that I was not sacked from
Clifton.'

Gethryn with some difficulty refrained from thanking him for the information.

'I never stop at a school long,' said Farnie. 'If I don't get sacked my father takes me away after a couple of terms. I went to four private schools before I started on the public schools. My pater took me away from the first two because he thought the drains were bad, the third because they wouldn't teach me shorthand, and the fourth because he didn't like the headmaster's face. I worked off those schools in a year and a half.' Having finished this piece of autobiography, he relapsed into silence, leaving Gethryn to recollect various tales he had heard of his grandfather's eccentricity. The silence lasted until the College was reached, when the matron took charge of Farnie, and Gethryn went off to tell Marriott of these strange happenings.

Marriott was amused, nor did he attempt to conceal the fact. When he had finished laughing, which was not for some time, he favoured the Bishop with a very sound piece of advice. 'If I were you,' he said, 'I should try and hush this affair up. It's all fearfully funny, but I think you'd enjoy life more if nobody knew this kid was your uncle. To see the head of the House going about with a juvenile uncle in his wake might amuse the chaps rather, and you might find it harder to keep order; I won't let it out, and nobody else knows apparently. Go and square the kid. Oh, I say though, what's his name? If it's Gethryn, you're done. Unless you like to swear he's a cousin.'

'No; his name's Farnie, thank goodness.'

'That's all right then. Go and talk to him.'

Gethryn went to the junior study. Farnie was holding forth to a knot of fags at one end of the room. His audience appeared to be amused at something.

'I say, Farnie,' said the Bishop, 'half a second.'

Farnie came out, and Gethryn proceeded to inform him that, all things considered, and proud as he was of the relationship, it was not absolutely essential that he should tell everybody that he was his uncle. In fact, it would be rather better on the whole if he did not. Did he follow?

Farnie begged to observe that he did follow, but that, to his sorrow, the warning came too late.

'I'm very sorry,' he said, 'I hadn't the least idea you wanted the thing kept dark. How was I to know? I've just been telling it to some of the chaps in there. Awfully decent chaps. They seemed to think it rather funny. Anyhow, I'm not ashamed of the relationship. Not yet, at any rate.'

For a moment Gethryn seemed about to speak. He looked fixedly at his uncle as he stood framed in the doorway, a cheerful column of cool, calm, concentrated cheek. Then, as if realizing that no words that he knew could do justice to the situation, he raised his foot in silence, and 'booted' his own flesh and blood with marked emphasis. After which ceremony he went, still without a word, upstairs again.

As for Farnie, he returned to the junior day-room whistling 'Down South' in a soft but cheerful key, and solidified his growing popularity with doles of food from a hamper which he had brought with him. Finally, on retiring to bed and being pressed by the rest of his dormitory for a story, he embarked upon the history of a certain Pollock and an individual referred to throughout as the Porroh Man, the former of whom caused the latter to be decapitated, and was ever afterwards haunted by his head, which appeared to him all day and every day (not excepting Sundays and Bank Holidays) in an upside-down position and wearing a horrible grin. In the end Pollock very sensibly committed suicide (with ghastly details), and the dormitory thanked Farnie in a subdued and chastened manner, and tried, with small success, to go to sleep. In short, Farnie's first evening at Beckford had been quite a triumph.

[4]

PRINGLE MAKES A SPORTING OFFER

Estimating it roughly, it takes a new boy at a public school about a week to find his legs and shed his skin of newness. The period is, of course, longer in the case of some and shorter in the case of others. Both Farnie and Wilson had made themselves at home immediately. In the case of the latter, directly the Skinner episode had been noised abroad, and it was discovered in addition that he was a promising bat, public opinion recognized that here was a youth out of the common run of new boys, and the Lower Fourth—the form in which he had been placed on arrival—took him to its bosom as an equal. Farnie's case was exceptional. A career at Harrow, Clifton, and Wellington, however short and abruptly terminated, gives one some sort of grip on the way public school life is conducted. At an early date, moreover, he gave signs of what almost amounted to genius in the Indoor Game department. Now, success in the field is a good thing, and undoubtedly makes for popularity. But if you desire to command the respect and admiration of your fellow-beings to a degree stretched almost to the point of idolatry, make yourself proficient in the art of whiling away the hours of afternoon school. Before Farnie's arrival, his form, the Upper Fourth, with the best intentions in the world, had not been skilful 'raggers'. They had ragged in an intermittent, once-a-week sort of way. When, however, he came on the scene, he introduced a welcome element of science into the sport. As witness the following. Mr Strudwick, the regular master of the form, happened on one occasion to be away for a couple of days, and a stop-gap was put in in his place. The name of the stop-gap was Mr Somerville Smith. He and Farnie exchanged an unspoken declaration of war almost immediately. The first round went in Mr Smith's favour. He contrived to catch Farnie in the act of performing some ingenious breach of the peace, and, it being a Wednesday and a half-holiday, sent him into extra lesson. On the following morning, more by design than accident, Farnie upset an inkpot. Mr Smith observed icily that unless the stain was wiped away before the beginning of afternoon school, there would be trouble. Farnie observed (to himself) that there would be trouble in any case, for he had hit upon the central idea for the most colossal 'rag' that, in his opinion, ever was. After morning school he gathered the form around him, and disclosed his idea. The floor of the form-room, he pointed out, was some dozen inches below the level of the door. Would it not be a pleasant and profitable notion, he asked, to flood the floor with water to the depth of those dozen inches? On the wall outside the form-room hung a row of buckets, placed there in case of fire, and the lavatory was not too far off for practical purposes. Mr Smith had bidden him wash the floor. It was obviously his duty to do so. The form thought so too. For a solid hour, thirty weary but enthusiastic reprobates laboured without ceasing, and by the time the bell rang all was prepared. The floor was one still, silent pool. Two caps and a few notebooks floated sluggishly on the surface, relieving the picture of any tendency to monotony. The form crept silently to their places along the desks. As Mr Smith's footsteps were heard approaching, they began to beat vigorously upon the desks, with the result that Mr Smith, quickening his pace, dashed into the form-room at a hard gallop. The immediate results were absolutely satisfactory, and if matters subsequently (when Mr Smith, having changed his clothes, returned with the Headmaster) did get somewhat warm for the thirty criminals, they had the satisfying feeling that their duty had been done, and a hearty and unanimous vote of thanks was passed to Farnie.

From which it will be seen that Master Reginald Farnie was managing to extract more or less enjoyment out of his life at Beckford.

Another person who was enjoying life was Pringle of the School House. The keynote of Pringle's character was superiority. At an early period of his life—he was still unable to speak at the time—his grandmother had died. This is probably the sole reason why he had never taught that relative to suck eggs. Had she lived, her education in that direction must have been taken in hand. Baffled in this, Pringle had turned his attention to the rest of the human race. He had a rooted conviction that he did everything a shade better than anybody else. This belief did not make him arrogant at all, and certainly not offensive, for he was exceedingly popular in the School. But still there were people who thought that he might occasionally draw the line somewhere. Watson, the ground-man, for example, thought so when Pringle primed him with advice on the subject of preparing a wicket. And Langdale, who had been captain of the team five years before, had thought so most decidedly, and had not hesitated to say so when Pringle, then in his first term and aged twelve, had stood behind the First Eleven net and requested him peremptorily to 'keep 'em down, sir, keep 'em down'. Indeed, the great man had very nearly had a fit on that occasion, and was wont afterwards to attribute to the effects of the shock so received a sequence of three 'ducks' which befell him in the next three matches.

In short, in every department of life, Pringle's advice was always (and generally unsought) at everybody's disposal. To round the position off neatly, it would be necessary to picture him as a total failure in the practical side of all the subjects in which he was so brilliant a theorist. Strangely enough, however, this was not the case. There were few better bats in the School than Pringle. Norris on his day was more stylish, and Marriott not infrequently made more runs, but for consistency Pringle was unrivalled.

That was partly the reason why at this time he was feeling pleased with life. The School had played three matches up to date, and had won them all. In the first, an Oxford college team, containing several Old Beckfordians, had been met and routed, Pringle contributing thirty-one to a total of three hundred odd. But Norris had made a century, which had rather diverted the public eye from this performance. Then the School had played the Emeriti, and had won again quite comfortably. This time his score had been forty-one, useful, but still not phenomenal. Then in the third match, *versus* Charchester, one of the big school matches of the season, he had found himself. He ran up a hundred and twenty-three without a chance, and felt that life had little more to offer. That had been only a week ago, and the glow of satisfaction was still pleasantly warm.

It was while he was gloating silently in his study over the bat with which a grateful Field Sports Committee had presented him as a reward for this feat, that he became aware that Lorimer, his study companion, appeared to be in an entirely different frame of mind to his own. Lorimer was in the Upper Fifth, Pringle in the Remove. Lorimer sat at the study table gnawing a pen in a feverish manner that told of an overwrought soul. Twice he uttered sounds that were obviously sounds of anguish, half groans and half grunts. Pringle laid down his bat and decided to investigate.

'What's up?' he asked.

'This bally poem thing,' said Lorimer.

'Poem? Oh, ah, I know.' Pringle had been in the Upper Fifth himself a year before, and he remembered that every summer term there descended upon that form a Bad Time in the shape of a poetry prize. A certain Indian potentate, the Rajah of Seltzerpore, had paid a visit to the school some years back, and had left behind him on his departure certain monies in the local bank, which were to be devoted to providing the Upper Fifth with an annual prize for the best poem on a subject to be selected by the Headmaster. Entrance was compulsory. The wily authorities knew very well that if it had not been, the entries for the prize would have been somewhat small. Why the Upper Fifth were so favoured in preference to the Sixth or Remove is doubtful. Possibly it was felt that, what with the Jones History, the Smith Latin Verse, the Robinson Latin Prose, and the De Vere Crespigny Greek Verse, and other trophies open only to members of the Remove and Sixth, those two forms had enough to keep them occupied as it was. At any rate, to the Upper Fifth the prize was given, and every year, three weeks after the commencement of the summer term, the Bad Time arrived.

'Can't you get on?' asked Pringle.

'No.'

'What's the subject?'

'Death of Dido.'

'Something to be got out of that, surely.'

'Wish you'd tell me what.'

'Heap of things.'

'Such as what? Can't see anything myself. I call it perfectly indecent dragging the good lady out of her well-earned tomb at this time of day. I've looked her up in the Dic. of Antiquities, and it appears that she committed suicide some years ago. Body-snatching, I call it. What do I want to know about her?'

'What's Hecuba to him or he to Hecuba?' murmured Pringle.

'Hecuba?' said Lorimer, looking puzzled, 'What's Hecuba got to do with it?'

'I was only quoting,' said Pringle, with gentle superiority.

'Well, I wish instead of quoting rot you'd devote your energies to helping me with these beastly verses. How on earth shall I begin?'

'You might adapt my quotation. "What's Dido got to do with me, or I to do with Dido?" I rather like that. Jam it down. Then you go on in a sort of rag-time metre. In the "Coon Drum-Major" style. Besides, you see, the beauty of it is that you administer a wholesome snub to the examiner right away. Makes him sit up at once. Put it down.'

Lorimer bit off another quarter of an inch of his pen. 'You needn't be an ass,' he said shortly.

'My dear chap,' said Pringle, enjoying himself immensely, 'what on earth is the good of my offering you suggestions if you won't take them?'

Lorimer said nothing. He bit off another mouthful of penholder.

'Well, anyway,' resumed Pringle. 'I can't see why you're so keen on the business. Put down anything. The beaks never make a fuss about these special exams.'

'It isn't the beaks I care about,' said Lorimer in an injured tone of voice, as if someone had been insinuating that he had committed some crime, 'only my people are rather keen on my doing well in this exam.'

'Why this exam, particularly?'

'Oh, I don't know. My grandfather or someone was a bit of a pro at verse in his day, I believe, and they think it ought to run in the family.'

Pringle examined the situation in all its aspects. 'Can't you get along?' he enquired at length.

'Not an inch.'

'Pity. I wish we could swop places.'

'So do I for some things. To start with, I shouldn't mind having made that century of yours against Charchester.'

Pringle beamed. The least hint that his fellow-man was taking him at his own valuation always made him happy.

'Thanks,' he said. 'No, but what I meant was that I wished I was in for this poetry prize. I bet I could turn out a rattling good screed. Why, last year I almost got the prize. I sent in fearfully hot stuff.'

'Think so?' said Lorimer doubtfully, in answer to the 'rattling good screed' passage of Pringle's speech. 'Well, I wish you'd have a shot. You might as well.'

'What, really? How about the prize?'

'Oh, hang the prize. We'll have to chance that.'

'I thought you were keen on getting it.'

'Oh, no. Second or third will do me all right, and satisfy my people. They only want to know for certain that I've got the poetic afflatus all right. Will you take it on?'

'All right.'

'Thanks, awfully.'

'I say, Lorimer,' said Pringle after a pause.

'Yes?'

'Are your people coming down for the O.B.s' match?'

The Old Beckfordians' match was the great function of the Beckford cricket season. The Headmaster gave a garden-party. The School band played; the School choir sang; and sisters, cousins, aunts, and parents flocked to the School in platoons.

'Yes, I think so,' said Lorimer. 'Why?'

'Is your sister coming?'

'Oh, I don't know.' A brother's utter lack of interest in his sister's actions is a weird and wonderful thing for an outsider to behold.

'Well, look here, I wish you'd get her to come. We could give them tea in here, and have rather a good time, don't you think?'

'All right. I'll make her come. Look here, Pringle, I believe you're rather gone on Mabel.'

This was Lorimer's vulgar way.

'Don't be an ass,' said Pringle, with a laugh which should have been careless, but was in reality merely feeble. 'She's quite a kid.'

Miss Mabel Lorimer's exact age was fifteen. She had brown hair, blue eyes, and a smile which disclosed to view a dimple. There are worse things than a dimple. Distinctly so, indeed. When ladies of fifteen possess dimples, mere man becomes but as a piece of damp blotting-paper. Pringle was seventeen and a half, and consequently too old to take note of such frivolous attributes; but all the same he had a sort of vague, sketchy

24

impression that it would be pleasanter to run up a lively century against the O.B.s with Miss Lorimer as a spectator than in her absence. He felt pleased that she was coming.

'I say, about this poem,' said Lorimer, dismissing a subject which manifestly bored him, and returning to one which was of vital interest, 'you're sure you can write fairly decent stuff? It's no good sending in stuff that'll turn the examiner's hair grey. Can you turn out something really decent?'

Pringle said nothing. He smiled gently as who should observe, 'I and

Shakespeare.'

[5]

FARNIE GETS INTO TROUBLE—

It was perhaps only natural that Farnie, having been warned so strongly of the inadvisability of having anything to do with Monk, should for that very reason be attracted to him. Nobody ever wants to do anything except what they are not allowed to do. Otherwise there is no explaining the friendship that arose between them. Jack Monk was not an attractive individual. He had a slack mouth and a shifty eye, and his complexion was the sort which friends would have described as olive, enemies (with more truth) as dirty green. These defects would have mattered little, of course, in themselves. There's many a bilious countenance, so to speak, covers a warm heart. With Monk, however, appearances were not deceptive. He looked a bad lot, and he was one.

It was on the second morning of term that the acquaintanceship began. Monk was coming downstairs from his study with Danvers, and Farnie was leaving the fags' day-room.

'See that kid?' said Danvers. 'That's the chap I was telling you about.

Gethryn's uncle, you know.'

'Not really? Let's cultivate him. I say, old chap, don't walk so fast.' Farnie, rightly concluding that the remark was addressed to him, turned and waited, and the three strolled over to the School buildings together.

They would have made an interesting study for the observer of human nature, the two seniors fancying that they had to deal with a small boy just arrived at his first school, and in the grip of that strange, lost feeling which attacks the best of new boys for a day or so after their arrival; and Farnie, on the other hand, watching every move, as perfectly composed and at home as a youth should be with the experience of three public schools to back him up.

When they arrived at the School gates, Monk and Danvers turned to go in the direction of their form-room, the Remove, leaving Farnie at the door of the Upper Fourth. At this point a small comedy took place. Monk, after feeling hastily in his pockets, requested Danvers to lend him five shillings until next Saturday. Danvers knew this request of old, and he knew the answer that was expected of him. By replying that he was sorry, but he had not got the money, he gave Farnie, who was still standing at the door, his cue to offer to supply the deficiency. Most new boys—they had grasped this fact from experience— would have felt it an honour to oblige a senior with a small loan. As Farnie made no signs of doing what was expected of him, Monk was obliged to resort to the somewhat cruder course of applying for the loan in person. He applied. Farnie with the utmost willingness brought to light a handful of money, mostly gold. Monk's eye gleamed approval, and he stretched forth an itching palm. Danvers began to think that it would be rash to let a chance like this slip. Ordinarily the tacit agreement between the pair was that only one should borrow at a time, lest confidence should be destroyed in the victim. But here was surely an exception, a special case. With a young gentleman so obviously a man of coin as Farnie, the rule might well be broken for once.

'While you're about it, Farnie, old man,' he said carelessly, 'you might let me have a bob or two if you don't mind. Five bob'll see me through to Saturday all right.'

'Do you mean tomorrow?' enquired Farnie, looking up from his heap of gold.

'No, Saturday week. Let you have it back by then at the latest. Make a point of it.'

'How would a quid do?'

'Ripping,' said Danvers ecstatically.

'Same here,' assented Monk.

'Then that's all right,' said Farnie briskly; 'I thought perhaps you mightn't have had enough. You've got a quid, I know, Monk, because I saw you haul one out at breakfast. And Danvers has got one too, because he offered to toss you for it in the study afterwards. And besides, I couldn't lend you anything in any case, because I've only got about fourteen quid myself.'

With which parting shot he retired, wrapped in gentle thought, into his form-room; and from the noise which ensued immediately upon his arrival, the shrewd listener would have deduced, quite correctly, that he had organized and taken the leading part in a general rag.

Monk and Danvers proceeded upon their way.

'You got rather left there, old chap,' said Monk at length.

'I like that,' replied the outraged Danvers. 'How about you, then? It seemed to me you got rather left, too.'

Monk compromised.

'Well, anyhow,' he said, 'we shan't get much out of that kid.'

'Little beast,' said Danvers complainingly. And they went on into their form-room in silence.

'I saw your young—er—relative in earnest conversation with friend Monk this morning,' said Marriott, later on in the day, to Gethryn; 'I thought you were going to give him the tip in that direction?'

'So I did,' said the Bishop wearily; 'but I can't always be looking after the little brute. He only does it out of sheer cussedness, because I've told him not to. It stands to reason that he can't *like* Monk.'

'You remind me of the psalmist and the wicked man, surname unknown,' said Marriott. 'You *can't* see the good side of Monk.'

'There isn't one.'

'No. He's only got two sides, a bad side and a worse side, which he sticks on on the strength of being fairly good at games. I wonder if he's going to get his First this season. He's not a bad bat.'

'I don't think he will. He is a good bat, but there are heaps better in the place. I say, I think I shall give young Farnie the tip once more, and let him take it or leave it. What do you think?'

'He'll leave it,' said Marriott, with conviction.

Nor was he mistaken. Farnie listened with enthusiasm to his nephew's second excursus on the Monk topic, and, though he said nothing, was apparently convinced. On the following afternoon Monk, Danvers, Waterford, and he hired a boat and went up the river together. Gethryn and Marriott, steered by Wilson, who was rapidly developing into a useful coxswain, got an excellent view of them moored under the shade of a willow, drinking ginger-beer, and apparently on the best of terms with one another and the world in general. In a brief but moving speech the Bishop finally excommunicated his erring relative.

'For all I care,' he concluded, 'he can do what he likes in future. I shan't stop him.'

'No,' said Marriott, 'I don't think you will.'

For the first month of his school life Farnie behaved, except in his choice of companions, much like an ordinary junior. He played cricket moderately well, did his share of compulsory fielding at the First Eleven net, and went for frequent river excursions with Monk, Danvers, and the rest of the Mob.

At first the other juniors of the House were inclined to resent this extending of the right hand of fellowship to owners of studies and Second Eleven men, and attempted to make Farnie see the sin and folly of his ways. But Nature had endowed that youth with a fund of vitriolic repartee. When Millett, one of Leicester's juniors, evolved some laborious sarcasm on the subject of Farnie's swell friends, Farnie, in a series of three remarks, reduced him, figuratively speaking, to a small and palpitating spot of grease. After that his actions came in for no further, or at any rate no outspoken comment.

Given sixpence a week and no more, Farnie might have survived an entire term without breaking any serious School rule. But when, after buying a bicycle from Smith of Markham's, he found himself with eight pounds to his name in solid cash, and the means of getting far enough away from the neighbourhood of the School to be able to spend it much as he liked, he began to do strange and risky things in his spare time.

The great obstacle to illicit enjoyment at Beckford was the four o'clock roll-call on half-holidays. There were other obstacles, such as half-holiday games and so forth, but these could be avoided by the exercise of a little judgement. The penalty for non-appearance at a half-holiday game was a fine of sixpence. Constant absence was likely in time to lead to a more or less thrilling interview with the captain of cricket, but a very occasional attendance was enough to stave off this disaster; and as for the sixpence, to a man of means like Farnie it was a mere nothing. It was a bad system, and it was a wonder, under the circumstances, how Beckford produced the elevens it did. But it was the system, and Farnie availed himself of it to the full.

The obstacle of roll-call he managed also to surmount. Some reckless and penniless friend was generally willing, for a consideration, to answer his name for him. And so most Saturday afternoons would find Farnie leaving behind him the flannelled fools at their various wickets, and speeding out into the country on his bicycle in the direction of the village of Biddlehampton, where mine host of the 'Cow and Cornflower', in addition to other refreshment for man and beast, advertised that ping-pong and billiards might be played on the premises. It was not the former of these games that attracted Farnie. He was no pinger. Nor was he a pongster. But for billiards he had a decided taste, a genuine taste, not the pumped-up affectation sometimes displayed by boys of his age. Considering his age he was a remarkable player. Later on in life it appeared likely that he would have the choice of three professions open to him, namely, professional billiard player, billiard marker, and billiard sharp. At each of the three he showed distinct promise. He was not 'lured to the green cloth' by Monk or Danvers. Indeed, if there had been any luring to be done, it is probable that he would have done it, and not they. Neither Monk nor Danvers was in his confidence in the matter. Billiards is not a cheap amusement. By the end of his sixth week Farnie was reduced to a single pound, a sum which, for one of his tastes, was practically poverty. And just at the moment when he was least able to bear up against it, Fate dealt him one of its nastiest blows. He was playing a fifty up against a friendly but unskilful farmer at the 'Cow and Cornflower'. 'Better look out,' he said, as his opponent effected a somewhat rustic stroke, 'you'll be cutting the cloth in a second.' The farmer grunted, missed by inches, and retired, leaving the red ball in the jaws of the pocket, and Farnie with three to make to win.

It was an absurdly easy stroke, and the Bishop's uncle took it with an absurd amount of conceit and carelessness. Hardly troubling to aim, he struck his ball. The cue slid off in one direction, the ball rolled sluggishly in another. And when the cue had finished its run, the smooth green surface of the table was marred by a jagged and unsightly cut. There was another young man gone wrong!

To say that the farmer laughed would be to express the matter feebly. That his young opponent, who had been irritating him unspeakably since the beginning of the game with advice and criticism, should have done exactly what he had cautioned him, the farmer, against a moment before, struck him as being the finest example of poetic justice he had ever heard of, and he signalized his appreciation of the same by nearly dying of apoplexy.

The marker expressed an opinion that Farnie had been and gone and done it.

"Ere,' he said, inserting a finger in the cut to display its dimensions. 'Look 'ere. This'll mean a noo cloth, young feller me

29

lad. That's wot this'll mean. That'll be three pound we will trouble you for, if *you* please.'

Farnie produced his sole remaining sovereign.

'All I've got,' he said. 'I'll leave my name and address.'

'Don't you trouble, young feller me lad,' said the marker, who appeared to be a very aggressive and unpleasant sort of character altogether, with meaning, 'I know yer name and I knows yer address. Today fortnight at the very latest, if *you* please. You don't want me to 'ave to go to your master about it, now, do yer? What say? No. Ve' well then. Today fortnight is the time, and you remember it.'

What was left of Farnie then rode slowly back to Beckford. Why he went to Monk on his return probably he could not have explained himself. But he did go, and, having told his story in full, wound up by asking for a loan of two pounds. Monk's first impulse was to refer him back to a previous interview, when matters had been the other way about, that small affair of the pound on the second morning of the term. Then there flashed across his mind certain reasons against this move. At present Farnie's attitude towards him was unpleasantly independent. He made him understand that he went about with him from choice, and that there was to be nothing of the patron and dependant about their alliance. If he were to lend him the two pounds now, things would alter. And to have got a complete hold over Master Reginald Farnie, Monk would have paid more than two pounds. Farnie had the intelligence to carry through anything, however risky, and there were many things which Monk would have liked to do, but, owing to the risks involved, shirked doing for himself. Besides, he happened to be in funds just now.

'Well, look here, old chap,' he said, 'let's have strict business between friends. If you'll pay me back four quid at the end of term, you shall have the two pounds. How does that strike you?'

It struck Farnie, as it would have struck most people, that if this was Monk's idea of strict business, there were the makings of no ordinary financier in him. But to get his two pounds he would have agreed to anything. And the end of term seemed a long way off.

The awkward part of the billiard-playing episode was that the punishment for it, if detected, was not expulsion, but flogging. And Farnie resembled the lady in *The Ingoldsby Legends* who 'didn't mind death, but who couldn't stand pinching'. He didn't mind expulsion—he was used to it, but he could *not* stand flogging.

'That'll be all right,' he said. And the money changed hands.

[6]

—AND STAYS THERE

'I say,' said Baker of Jephson's excitedly some days later, reeling into the study which he shared with Norris, '*have* you seen the team the M.C.C.'s bringing down?'

At nearly every school there is a type of youth who asks this question on the morning of the M.C.C. match. Norris was engaged in putting the finishing touches to a snow-white pair of cricket boots.

'No. Hullo, where did you raise that Sporter? Let's have a look.'

But Baker proposed to conduct this business in person. It is ten times more pleasant to administer a series of shocks to a friend than to sit by and watch him administering them to himself. He retained *The Sportsman*, and began to read out the team.

'Thought Middlesex had a match,' said Norris, as Baker paused dramatically to let the name of a world-famed professional sink in.

'No. They don't play Surrey till Monday.'

'Well, if they've got an important match like Surrey on on Monday,' said Norris disgustedly, 'what on earth do they let their best man come down here today for, and fag himself out?'

Baker suggested gently that if anybody was going to be fagged out at the end of the day, it would in all probability be the Beckford bowlers, and not a man who, as he was careful to point out, had run up a century a mere three days ago against Yorkshire, and who was apparently at that moment at the very top of his form.

'Well,' said Norris, 'he might crock himself or anything. Rank bad policy, I call it. Anybody else?'

Baker resumed his reading. A string of unknowns ended in another celebrity.

'Blackwell?' said Norris. 'Not O. T. Blackwell?'

'It says A. T. But,' went on Baker, brightening up again, 'they always get the initials wrong in the papers. Certain to be O. T. By the way, I suppose you saw that he made eighty-three against Notts the other day?'

Norris tried to comfort himself by observing that Notts couldn't bowl for toffee.

31

'Last week, too,' said Baker, 'he made a hundred and forty-six not out against Malvern for the Gentlemen of Warwickshire. They couldn't get him out,' he concluded with unction. In spite of the fact that he himself was playing in the match today, and might under the circumstances reasonably look forward to a considerable dose of leather-hunting, the task of announcing the bad news to Norris appeared to have a most elevating effect on his spirits:

'That's nothing extra special,' said Norris, in answer to the last item of information, 'the Malvern wicket's like a billiard-table.'

'Our wickets aren't bad either at this time of year,' said Baker, 'and

I heard rumours that they had got a record one ready for this match.'

'It seems to me,' said Norris, 'that what I'd better do if we want to bat at all today is to win the toss. Though Sammy and the Bishop and Baynes ought to be able to get any ordinary side out all right.'

'Only this isn't an ordinary side. It's a sort of improved county team.'

'They've got about four men who might come off, but the M.C.C. sometimes have a bit of a tail. We ought to have a look in if we win the toss.'

'Hope so,' said Baker. 'I doubt it, though.'

At a quarter to eleven the School always went out in a body to inspect the pitch. After the wicket had been described by experts in hushed whispers as looking pretty good, the bell rang, and all who were not playing for the team, with the exception of the lucky individual who had obtained for himself the post of scorer, strolled back towards the blocks. Monk had come out with Waterford, but seeing Farnie ahead and walking alone he quitted Waterford, and attached himself to the genial Reginald. He wanted to talk business. He had not found the speculation of the two pounds a very profitable one. He had advanced the money under the impression that Farnie, by accepting it, was practically selling his independence. And there were certain matters in which Monk was largely interested, connected with the breaking of bounds and the purchase of contraband goods, which he would have been exceedingly glad to have performed by deputy. He had fancied that Farnie would have taken over these jobs as part of his debt. But he had mistaken his man. On the very first occasion when he had attempted to put on the screw, Farnie had flatly refused to have anything to do with what he proposed. He said that he was not Monk's fag—a remark which had the merit of being absolutely true.

All this, combined with a slight sinking of his own funds, induced Monk to take steps towards recovering the loan.

'I say, Farnie, old chap.'

'Hullo!'

'I say, do you remember my lending you two quid some time ago?'

'You don't give me much chance of forgetting it,' said Farnie.

Monk smiled. He could afford to be generous towards such witticisms.

'I want it back,' he said.

'All right. You'll get it at the end of term.'

'I want it now.'

'Why?'

'Awfully hard up, old chap.'

'You aren't,' said Farnie. 'You've got three pounds twelve and sixpence half-penny. If you will keep counting your money in public, you can't blame a chap for knowing how much you've got.'

Monk, slightly disconcerted, changed his plan of action. He abandoned skirmishing tactics.

'Never mind that,' he said, 'the point is that I want that four pounds.

I'm going to have it, too.'

'I know. At the end of term.'

'I'm going to have it now.'

'You can have a pound of it now.'

'Not enough.'

'I don't see how you expect me to raise any more. If I could, do you think I should have borrowed it? You might chuck rotting for a change.'

'Now, look here, old chap,' said Monk, 'I should think you'd rather raise that tin somehow than have it get about that you'd been playing pills at some pub out of bounds. What?'

Farnie, for one of the few occasions on record, was shaken out of his usual *sang-froid*. Even in his easy code of morality there had always been one crime which was an anathema, the sort of thing no fellow could think of doing. But it was obviously at this that Monk was hinting.

'Good Lord, man,' he cried, 'you don't mean to say you're thinking of sneaking? Why, the fellows would boot you round the field. You couldn't stay in the place a week.'

'There are heaps of ways,' said Monk, 'in which a thing can get about without anyone actually telling the beaks. At present I've not told a soul. But, you know, if I let it out to anyone they might tell someone else, and so on. And if everybody knows a thing, the beaks generally get hold of it sooner or later. You'd much better let me have that four quid, old chap.'

Farnie capitulated.

'All right,' he said, 'I'll get it somehow.'

'Thanks awfully, old chap,' said Monk, 'so long!'

In all Beckford there was only one person who was in the least degree likely to combine the two qualities necessary for the extraction of Farnie from his difficulties. These qualities were— in the first place ability, in the second place willingness to advance him, free of security, the four pounds he required. The person whom he had in his mind was Gethryn. He had reasoned the matter out step by step during the second half of morning school. Gethryn, though he had, as Farnie knew, no overwhelming amount of affection for his uncle, might in a case of great need prove blood to be thicker (as per advertisement) than water. But, he reflected, he must represent himself as in danger of expulsion rather than flogging. He had an uneasy idea that if the Bishop were to discover that all he stood to get was a flogging, he would remark with enthusiasm that, as far as he was concerned, the good work might go on. Expulsion was different. To save a member of his family from expulsion, he might think it worth while to pass round the hat amongst his wealthy acquaintances. If four plutocrats with four sovereigns were to combine, Farnie, by their united efforts, would be saved. And he rather liked the notion of being turned into a sort of limited liability company, like the Duke of Plaza Toro, at a pound a share. It seemed to add a certain dignity to his position.

To Gethryn's study, therefore, he went directly school was over. If he had reflected, he might have known that he would not have been there while the match was going on. But his brain, fatigued with his recent calculations, had not noted this point.

The study was empty.

Most people, on finding themselves in a strange and empty room, are seized with a desire to explore the same, and observe from internal evidence what manner of man is the owner. Nowhere does character come out so clearly as in the decoration of one's private den. Many a man, at present respected by his associates, would stand forth unmasked at his true worth, could the world but look into his room. For there they would see that he was so lost to every sense of shame as to cover his books with brown paper, or deck his walls with oleographs presented with the Christmas numbers, both of which habits argue a frame of mind fit for murderers, stratagems, and spoils. Let no such man be trusted.

The Bishop's study, which Farnie now proceeded to inspect, was not of this kind. It was a neat study, arranged with not a little taste. There were photographs of teams with the College arms on their plain oak frames, and photographs of relations in frames which tried to look, and for the most part succeeded in looking, as if they had not cost fourpence three farthings at a Christmas bargain sale. There were snap-shots of various moving incidents in the careers of the Bishop and his friends: Marriott, for example, as he appeared when carried to the Pavilion after that sensational century against the Authentics: Robertson of Blaker's winning the quarter mile: John Brown, Norris's predecessor in the captaincy, and one of the four best batsmen Beckford had ever had, batting at the nets: Norris taking a skier on the boundary in last year's M.C.C. match: the Bishop himself going out to bat in the Charchester match, and many more of the same sort.

All these Farnie observed with considerable interest, but as he moved towards the book-shelf his eye was caught by an object more interesting still. It was a cash-box, simple and unornamental, but undoubtedly a cash-box, and as he took it up it rattled.

The key was in the lock. In a boarding House at a public school it is not, as a general rule, absolutely necessary to keep one's valuables always hermetically sealed. The difference between *meum* and *tuum* is so very rarely confused by the occupants of such an establishment, that one is apt to grow careless, and every now and then accidents happen. An accident was about to happen now.

It was at first without any motive except curiosity that Farnie opened the cash-box. He merely wished to see how much there was inside, with a view to ascertaining what his prospects of negotiating a loan with his relative were likely to be. When, however, he did see, other feelings began to take the place of curiosity. He counted the money. There were ten sovereigns, one half-sovereign, and a good deal of silver. One of the institutions at Beckford was a mission. The School by (more or less) voluntary contributions supported a species of home somewhere in the wilds of Kennington. No one knew exactly what or where this home was, but all paid their subscriptions as soon as possible in the term, and tried to forget about it. Gethryn collected not only for Leicester's House, but also for the Sixth Form, and was consequently, if only by proxy, a man of large means. *Too* large, Farnie thought. Surely four pounds, to be paid back (probably) almost at once, would not be missed. Why shouldn't he—

'Hullo!'

Farnie spun round. Wilson was standing in the doorway.

'Hullo, Farnie,' said he, 'what are you playing at in here?'

'What are you?' retorted Farnie politely.

'Come to fetch a book. Marriott said I might. What are you up to?'

'Oh, shut up!' said Farnie. 'Why shouldn't I come here if I like? Matter of fact, I came to see Gethryn.'

'He isn't here,' said Wilson luminously.

'You don't mean to say you've noticed that already? You've got an eye like a hawk, Wilson. I was just taking a look round, if you really want to know.'

'Well, I shouldn't advise you to let Marriott catch you mucking his study up. Seen a book called *Round the Red Lamp*? Oh, here it is. Coming over to the field?'

'Not just yet. I want to have another look round. Don't you wait, though.'

'Oh, all right.' And Wilson retired with his book.

Now, though Wilson at present suspected nothing, not knowing of the existence of the cash-box, Farnie felt that when the money came to be missed, and inquiries were made as to who had been in the study, and when, he would recall the interview. Two courses, therefore, remained open to him. He could leave the money altogether, or he could take it and leave himself. In other words, run away.

In the first case there would, of course, remain the chance that he might induce Gethryn to lend him the four pounds, but this had never been more than a forlorn hope; and in the light of the possibilities opened out by the cash-box, he thought no more of it. The real problem was, should he or should he not take the money from the cash-box?

As he hesitated, the recollection of Monk's veiled threats came back to him, and he wavered no longer. He opened the box again, took out the contents, and dropped them into his pocket. While he was about it, he thought he might as well take all as only a part.

Then he wrote two notes. One—to the Bishop—he placed on top of the cash-box; the other he placed with four sovereigns on the table in Monk's study. Finally he left the room, shut the door carefully behind him, and went to the yard at the back of the House, where he kept his bicycle.

The workings of the human mind, and especially of the young human mind, are peculiar. It never occurred to Farnie that a result equally profitable to himself, and decidedly more convenient for all concerned—with the possible exception of Monk—might have been arrived at if he had simply left the money in the box, and run away without it.

However, as the poet says, you can't think of everything.

[7]

THE BISHOP GOES FOR A RIDE

The M.C.C. match opened auspiciously. Norris, for the first time that season, won the toss. Tom Brown, we read, in a similar position, 'with the usual liberality of young hands', put his opponents in first. Norris was not so liberal. He may have been young, but he was not so young as that. The sun was shining on as true a wicket as was ever prepared when he cried 'Heads', and the coin, after rolling for some time in diminishing circles, came to a standstill with the dragon undermost. And Norris returned to the Pavilion and informed his gratified team that, all things considered, he rather thought that they would bat, and he would be obliged if Baker would get on his pads and come in first with him.

The M.C.C. men took the field—O. T. Blackwell, by the way, had shrunk into a mere brother of the century-making A. T.— and the two School House representatives followed them. An amateur of lengthy frame took the ball, a man of pace, to judge from the number of slips. Norris asked for 'two leg'. An obliging umpire informed him that he had got two leg. The long bowler requested short slip to stand finer, swung his arm as if to see that the machinery still worked, and dashed wildly towards the crease. The match had begun.

There are few pleasanter or more thrilling moments in one's school career than the first over of a big match. Pleasant, that is to say, if you are actually looking on. To have to listen to a match being started from the interior of a form-room is, of course, maddening. You hear the sound of bat meeting ball, followed by distant clapping. Somebody has scored. But who and what? It may be a four, or it may be a mere single. More important still, it may be the other side batting after all. Some miscreant has possibly lifted your best bowler into the road. The suspense is awful. It ought to be a School rule that the captain of the team should send a message round the form-rooms stating briefly and lucidly the result of the toss. Then one would know where one was. As it is, the entire form is dependent on the man sitting under the window. The form-master turns to write on the blackboard. The only hope of the form shoots up like a rocket, gazes earnestly in the direction of the Pavilion, and falls back with a thud into his seat. 'They haven't started yet,' he informs the rest in a stage whisper. 'Si-*lence*,' says the form-master, and the whole business must be gone through again, with the added disadvantage that the master now has his eye fixed coldly on the individual nearest the window, your only link with the outer world.

Various masters have various methods under such circumstances. One more than excellent man used to close his book and remark, 'I think we'll make up a little party to watch this match.' And the form, gasping its thanks, crowded to the windows. Another, the exact antithesis of this great and good gentleman, on seeing a boy taking fitful glances through the window, would observe acidly, 'You are at perfect liberty, Jones, to watch the match if you care to, but if you do you will come in in the afternoon and make up the time you waste.' And as all that could be seen from that particular window was one of the umpires and a couple of fieldsmen, Jones would reluctantly elect to reserve himself, and for the present to turn his attention to Euripides again.

If you are one of the team, and watch the match from the Pavilion, you escape these trials, but there are others. In the first few overs of a School match, every ball looks to the spectators like taking a wicket. The fiendish ingenuity of the slow bowler, and the lightning speed of the fast man at the other end, make one feel positively ill. When the first ten has gone up on the scoring-board matters begin to right themselves. Today ten went up quickly. The fast man's first ball was outside the off-stump and a half-volley, and Norris, whatever the state of his nerves at the time, never forgot his forward drive. Before the bowler had recovered his balance the ball was half-way to the ropes. The umpire waved a large hand towards the Pavilion. The bowler looked annoyed. And the School inside the form-rooms asked itself feverishly what had happened, and which side it was that was applauding.

Having bowled his first ball too far up, the M.C.C. man, on the principle of anything for a change, now put in a very short one. Norris, a new man after that drive, steered it through the slips, and again the umpire waved his hand.

The rest of the over was more quiet. The last ball went for four byes, and then it was Baker's turn to face the slow man. Baker was a steady, plodding bat. He played five balls gently to mid-on, and glanced the sixth for a single to leg. With the fast bowler, who had not yet got his length, he was more vigorous, and succeeded in cutting him twice for two.

With thirty up for no wickets the School began to feel more comfortable. But at forty-three Baker was shattered by the man of pace, and retired with twenty to his credit. Gethryn came in next, but it was not to be his day out with the bat.

The fast bowler, who was now bowling excellently, sent down one rather wide of the off-stump. The Bishop made most of his runs from off balls, and he had a go at this one. It was rising when he hit it, and it went off his bat like a flash. In a School match it would have been a boundary. But today there was unusual talent in the slips. The man from Middlesex darted forward and sideways. He took the ball one-handed two inches from the ground, and received the applause which followed the effort with a rather bored look, as if he were saying, 'My good sirs, *why* make a fuss over these trifles!' The Bishop walked slowly back to the Pavilion, feeling that his luck was out, and Pringle came in.

A boy of Pringle's character is exactly the right person to go in in an emergency like the present one. Two wickets had fallen in two balls, and the fast bowler was swelling visibly with determination to do the hat-trick. But Pringle never went in oppressed by the fear of getting out. He had a serene and boundless confidence in himself.

The fast man tried a yorker. Pringle came down hard on it, and forced the ball past the bowler for a single. Then he and Norris settled down to a lengthy stand.

'I do like seeing Pringle bat,' said Gosling. 'He always gives you the idea that he's doing you a personal favour by knocking your bowling about. Oh, well hit!'

Pringle had cut a full-pitch from the slow bowler to the ropes. Marriott, who had been silent and apparently in pain for some minutes, now gave out the following homemade effort:

A dashing young sportsman named Pringle,

On breaking his duck (with a single),
   Observed with a smile,
   'Just notice my style,
How science with vigour I mingle.'

'Little thing of my own,' he added, quoting England's greatest librettist. 'I call it "Heart Foam". I shall not publish it. Oh, run it out!'

Both Pringle and Norris were evidently in form. Norris was now not far from his fifty, and Pringle looked as if he might make anything. The century went up, and a run later Norris off-drove the slow bowler's successor for three, reaching his fifty by the stroke.

'Must be fairly warm work fielding today,' said Reece.

'By Jove!' said Gethryn, 'I forgot. I left my white hat in the House.

Any of you chaps like to fetch it?'

There were no offers. Gethryn got up.

'Marriott, you slacker, come over to the House.'

'My good sir, I'm in next. Why don't you wait till the fellows come out of school and send a kid for it?'

'He probably wouldn't know where to find it. I don't know where it is myself. No, I shall go, but there's no need to fag about it yet. Hullo! Norris is out.'

Norris had stopped a straight one with his leg. He had made fifty-one in his best manner, and the School, leaving the form-rooms at the exact moment when the fatal ball was being bowled, were just in time to applaud him and realize what they had missed.

Gethryn's desire for his hat was not so pressing as to make him deprive himself of the pleasure of seeing Marriott at the wickets. Marriott ought to do something special today. Unfortunately, after he had played out one over and hit two fours off it, the luncheon interval began.

It was, therefore, not for half an hour that the Bishop went at last in search of the missing headgear. As luck would have it, the hat was on the table, so that whatever chance he might have had of overlooking the note which his uncle had left for him on the empty cash-box disappeared. The two things caught his eye simultaneously. He opened the note and read it. It is not necessary to transcribe the note in detail. It was no masterpiece of literary skill. But it had this merit, that it was not vague. Reading it, one grasped its meaning immediately.

The Bishop's first feeling was that the bottom had dropped out of everything suddenly. Surprise was not the word. It was the arrival of the absolutely unexpected.

Then he began to consider the position.

Farnie must be brought back. That was plain. And he must be brought back at once, before anyone could get to hear of what had happened. Gethryn had the very strongest objections to his uncle, considered purely as a human being; but the fact remained that he was his uncle, and the Bishop had equally strong objections to any member of his family being mixed up in a business of this description.

Having settled that point, he went on to the next. How was he to be brought back? He could not have gone far, for he could not have been gone much more than half an hour. Again, from his knowledge of his uncle's character, he deduced that he had in all probability not gone to the nearest station, Horton. At Horton one had to wait hours at a time for a train. Farnie must have made his way—on his bicycle—straight for the junction, Anfield, fifteen miles off by a good road. A train left Anfield for London at three-thirty. It was now a little past two. On a bicycle he could do it easily, and get back with his prize by about five, if he rode hard. In that case all would be well. Only three of the School wickets had fallen, and the pitch was playing as true as concrete. Besides, there was Pringle still in at one end, well set, and surely Marriott and Jennings and the rest of them would manage to stay in till five. They couldn't help it. All they had to do was to play forward to everything, and they must stop in. He himself had got out, it was true, but that was simply a regrettable accident. Not one man in a hundred would have caught that catch. No, with luck he ought easily to be able to do the distance and get back in time to go out with the rest of the team to field.

He ran downstairs and out of the House. On his way to the bicycle-shed he stopped, and looked towards the field, part of which could be seen from where he stood. The match had begun again. The fast bowler was just commencing his run. He saw him tear up to the crease and deliver the ball. What happened then he could not see, owing to the trees which stood between him and the School grounds. But he heard the crack of ball meeting bat, and a great howl of applause went up from the invisible audience. A boundary, apparently. Yes, there was the umpire signalling it. Evidently a long stand was going to be made. He would have oceans of time for his ride. Norris wouldn't dream of declaring the innings closed before five o'clock at the earliest, and no

41

bowler could take seven wickets in the time on such a pitch. He hauled his bicycle from the shed, and rode off at racing speed in the direction of Anfield.

[8]

THE M.C.C. MATCH

But out in the field things were going badly with Beckford. The aspect of a game often changes considerably after lunch. For a while it looked as if Marriott and Pringle were in for their respective centuries. But Marriott was never a safe batsman.

A hundred and fifty went up on the board off a square leg hit for two, which completed Pringle's half-century, and then Marriott faced the slow bowler, who had been put on again after lunch. The first ball was a miss-hit. It went behind point for a couple. The next he got fairly hold of and drove to the boundary. The third was a very simple-looking ball. Its sole merit appeared to be the fact that it was straight. Also it was a trifle shorter than it looked. Marriott jumped out, and got too much under it. Up it soared, straight over the bowler's head. A trifle more weight behind the hit, and it would have cleared the ropes. As it was, the man in the deep-field never looked like missing it. The batsmen had time to cross over before the ball arrived, but they did it without enthusiasm. The run was not likely to count. Nor did it. Deep-field caught it like a bird. Marriott had made twenty-two.

And now occurred one of those rots which so often happen without any ostensible cause in the best regulated school elevens. Pringle played the three remaining balls of the over without mishap, but when it was the fast man's turn to bowl to Bruce, Marriott's successor, things began to happen. Bruce, temporarily insane, perhaps through nervousness, played back at a half-volley, and was clean bowled. Hill came in, and was caught two balls later at the wicket. And the last ball of the over sent Jennings's off-stump out of the ground, after that batsman had scored two.

'I can always bowl like blazes after lunch,' said the fast man to Pringle. 'It's the lobster salad that does it, I think.' Four for a hundred and fifty-seven had changed to seven for a hundred and fifty-nine in the course of a single over. Gethryn's calculations, if he had only known, could have done now with a little revision.

42

Gosling was the next man. He was followed, after a brief innings of three balls, which realized eight runs, by Baynes. Baynes, though abstaining from runs himself, helped Pringle to add three to the score, all in singles, and was then yorked by the slow man, who meanly and treacherously sent down, without the slightest warning, a very fast one on the leg stump. Then Reece came in for the last wicket, and the rot stopped. Reece always went in last for the School, and the School in consequence always felt that there were possibilities to the very end of the innings.

The lot of a last-wicket man is somewhat trying. As at any moment his best innings may be nipped in the bud by the other man getting out, he generally feels that it is hardly worth while to play himself in before endeavouring to make runs. He therefore tries to score off every ball, and thinks himself lucky if he gets half a dozen. Reece, however, took life more seriously. He had made quite an art of last-wicket batting. Once, against the Butterflies, he had run up sixty not out, and there was always the chance that he would do the same again. Today, with Pringle at the other end, he looked forward to a pleasant hour or two at the wicket.

No bowler ever looks on the last man quite in the same light as he does the other ten. He underrates him instinctively. The M.C.C. fast bowler was a man with an idea. His idea was that he could bowl a slow ball of diabolical ingenuity. As a rule, public feeling was against his trying the experiment. His captains were in the habit of enquiring rudely if he thought he was playing marbles. This was exactly what the M.C.C. captain asked on the present occasion, when the head ball sailed ponderously through the air, and was promptly hit by Reece into the Pavilion. The bowler grinned, and resumed his ordinary pace.

But everything came alike to Reece. Pringle, too, continued his career of triumph. Gradually the score rose from a hundred and seventy to two hundred. Pringle cut and drove in all directions, with the air of a prince of the blood royal distributing largesse. The second century went up to the accompaniment of cheers.

Then the slow bowler reaped his reward, for Pringle, after putting his first two balls over the screen, was caught on the boundary off the third. He had contributed eighty-one to a total of two hundred and thirteen.

So far Gethryn's absence had not been noticed. But when the umpires had gone out, and the School were getting ready to take the field, inquiries were made.

'You might begin at the top end, Gosling,' said Norris.

43

'Right,' said Samuel. 'Who's going on at the other?'

'Baynes. Hullo, where's Gethryn?'

'Isn't he here? Perhaps he's in the Pavi—'

'Any of you chaps seen Gethryn?'

'He isn't in the Pav.,' said Baker. 'I've just come out of the First room myself, and he wasn't there. Shouldn't wonder if he's over at Leicester's.'

'Dash the man,' said Norris, 'he might have known we'd be going out to field soon. Anyhow, we can't wait for him. We shall have to field a sub. till he turns up.'

'Lorimer's in the Pav., changed,' said Pringle.

'All right. He'll do.'

And, reinforced by the gratified Lorimer, the team went on its way.

In the beginning the fortunes of the School prospered. Gosling opened, as was his custom, at a tremendous pace, and seemed to trouble the first few batsmen considerably. A worried-looking little person who had fielded with immense zeal during the School innings at cover-point took the first ball. It was very fast, and hit him just under the knee-cap. The pain, in spite of the pad, appeared to be acute. The little man danced vigorously for some time, and then, with much diffidence, prepared himself for the second instalment.

Now, when on the cricket field, the truculent Samuel was totally deficient in all the finer feelings, such as pity and charity. He could see that the batsman was in pain, and yet his second ball was faster than the first. It came in quickly from the off. The little batsman went forward in a hesitating, half-hearted manner, and played a clear two inches inside the ball. The off-stump shot out of the ground.

'Bowled, Sammy,' said Norris from his place in the slips.

The next man was a clergyman, a large man who suggested possibilities in the way of hitting. But Gosling was irresistible. For three balls the priest survived. But the last of the over, a fast yorker on the leg stump, was too much for him, and he retired.

Two for none. The critic in the deck chair felt that the match was as good as over.

But this idyllic state of things was not to last. The newcomer, a tall man with a light moustache, which he felt carefully after every ball, soon settled down. He proved to be a conversationalist. Until he had opened his account, which he did with a strong drive to the ropes, he was silent. When, however, he had seen the ball safely to the boundary, he turned to Reece and began.

'Rather a nice one, that. Eh, what? Yes. Got it just on the right place, you know. Not a bad bat this, is it? What? Yes. One of Slogbury and Whangham's Sussex Spankers, don't you know. Chose it myself. Had it in pickle all the winter. Yes.'

'Play, sir,' from the umpire.

'Eh, what? Oh, right. Yes, good make these Sussex—*Spankers*. Oh, well fielded.'

At the word spankers he had effected another drive, but Marriott at mid-off had stopped it prettily.

Soon it began to occur to Norris that it would be advisable to have a change of bowling. Gosling was getting tired, and Baynes apparently offered no difficulties to the batsman on the perfect wicket, the conversational man in particular being very severe upon him. It was at such a crisis that the Bishop should have come in. He was Gosling's understudy. But where was he? The innings had been in progress over half an hour now, and still there were no signs of him. A man, thought Norris, who could cut off during the M.C.C. match (of all matches!), probably on some rotten business of his own, was beyond the pale, and must, on reappearance, be fallen upon and rent. He—here something small and red whizzed at his face. He put up his hands to protect himself. The ball struck them and bounded out again. When a fast bowler is bowling a slip he should not indulge in absent-mindedness. The conversational man had received his first life, and, as he was careful to explain to Reece, it was a curious thing, but whenever he was let off early in his innings he always made fifty, and as a rule a century. Gosling's analysis was spoilt, and the match in all probability lost. And Norris put it all down to Gethryn. If he had been there, this would not have happened.

'Sorry, Gosling,' he said.

'All right,' said Gosling, though thinking quite the reverse. And he walked back to bowl his next ball, conjuring up a beautiful vision in his mind. J. Douglas and Braund were fielding slip to him in the vision, while in the background Norris appeared, in a cauldron of boiling oil.

'Tut, tut,' said Baker facetiously to the raging captain.

Baker's was essentially a flippant mind. Not even a moment of solemn agony, such as this, was sacred to him.

Norris was icy and severe.

'If you want to rot about, Baker,' he said, 'perhaps you'd better go and play stump-cricket with the juniors.'

'Well,' retorted Baker, with great politeness, 'I suppose seeing you miss a gaper like that right into your hands made me think I was playing stump-cricket with the juniors.'

At this point the conversation ceased, Baker suddenly remembering that he had not yet received his First Eleven colours, and that it would therefore be rash to goad the captain too freely, while Norris, for his part, recalled the fact that Baker had promised to do some Latin verse for him that evening, and might, if crushed with some scathing repartee, refuse to go through with that contract. So there was silence in the slips.

The partnership was broken at last by a lucky accident. The conversationalist called his partner for a short run, and when that unfortunate gentleman had sprinted some twenty yards, reconsidered the matter and sent him back. Reece had the bails off before the victim had completed a third of the return journey.

For some time after this matters began to favour the School again. With the score at a hundred and five, three men left in two overs, one bowled by Gosling, the others caught at point and in the deep off Jennings, who had deposed Baynes. Six wickets were now down, and the enemy still over a hundred behind.

But the M.C.C. in its school matches has this peculiarity. However badly it may seem to stand, there is always something up its sleeve. In this case it was a professional, a man indecently devoid of anything in the shape of nerves. He played the bowling with a stolid confidence, amounting almost to contempt, which struck a chill to the hearts of the School bowlers. It did worse. It induced them to bowl with the sole object of getting the conversationalist at the batting end, thus enabling the professional to pile up an unassuming but rapidly increasing score by means of threes and singles.

As for the conversationalist, he had made thirty or more, and wanted all the bowling he could get.

'It's a very curious thing,' he said to Reece, as he faced Gosling, after his partner had scored a three off the first ball of the over, 'but some fellows simply detest fast bowling. Now I—' He never finished the sentence. When he spoke again it was to begin a new one.

'How on earth did that happen?' he asked.

'I think it bowled you,' said Reece stolidly, picking up the two stumps which had been uprooted by Gosling's express.

'Yes. But how? Dash it! What? I can't underst——. Most curious thing I ever—dash it all, you know.'

He drifted off in the direction of the Pavilion, stopping on the way to ask short leg his opinion of the matter.

'Bowled, Sammy,' said Reece, putting on the bails.

'Well bowled, Gosling,' growled Norris from the slips.

'Sammy the marvel, by Jove,' said Marriott. 'Switch it on, Samuel, more and more.'

'I wish Norris would give me a rest. Where on earth is that man

Gethryn?'

'Rum, isn't it? There's going to be something of a row about it. Norris seems to be getting rather shirty. Hullo! here comes the Deathless Author.'

The author referred to was the new batsman, a distinguished novelist, who played a good deal for the M.C.C. He broke his journey to the wicket to speak to the conversationalist, who was still engaged with short leg.

'Bates, old man,' he said, 'if you're going to the Pavilion you might wait for me. I shall be out in an hour or two.'

Upon which Bates, awaking suddenly to the position of affairs, went on his way.

With the arrival of the Deathless Author an unwelcome change came over the game. His cricket style resembled his literary style. Both were straightforward and vigorous. The first two balls he received from Gosling he drove hard past cover point to the ropes. Gosling, who had been bowling unchanged since the innings began, was naturally feeling a little tired. He was losing his length, and bowling more slowly than was his wont. Norris now gave him a rest for a few overs, Bruce going on with rather innocuous medium left-hand bowling. The professional continued to jog along slowly. The novelist hit. Everything seemed to come alike to him. Gosling resumed, but without effect, while at the other end bowler after bowler was tried. From a hundred and ten the score rose and rose, and still the two remained together. A hundred and ninety went up, and Norris in despair threw the ball to Marriott.

'Here you are, Marriott,' he said, 'I'm afraid we shall have to try you.'

'That's what I call really nicely expressed,' said Marriott to the umpire. 'Yes, over the wicket.'

Marriott was a slow, 'House-match' sort of bowler. That is to say, in a House match he was quite likely to get wickets, but in a First Eleven match such an event was highly improbable. His bowling looked very subtle, and if the ball was allowed to touch the ground it occasionally broke quite a remarkable distance.

The forlorn hope succeeded. The professional for the first time in his innings took a risk. He slashed at a very mild ball almost a wide on the off side. The ball touched the corner of the bat, and soared up in the direction of cover-point, where Pringle held it comfortably.

'There you are,' said Marriott, 'when you put a really scientific bowler on you're bound to get a wicket. Why on earth didn't I go on before, Norris?'

'You wait,' said Norris, 'there are five more balls of the over to come.'

'Bad job for the batsman,' said Marriott.

There had been time for a run before the ball reached Pringle, so that the novelist was now at the batting end. Marriott's next ball was not unlike his first, but it was straighter, and consequently easier to get at. The novelist hit it into the road. When it had been brought back he hit it into the road again. Marriott suggested that he had better have a man there.

The fourth ball of the over was too wide to hit with any comfort, and the batsman let it alone. The fifth went for four to square leg, almost killing the umpire on its way, and the sixth soared in the old familiar manner into the road again. Marriott's over had yielded exactly twenty-two runs. Four to win and two wickets to fall.

'I'll never read another of that man's books as long as I live,' said

Marriott to Gosling, giving him the ball. 'You're our only hope, Sammy.

Do go in and win.'

The new batsman had the bowling. He snicked his first ball for a single, bringing the novelist to the fore again, and Samuel Wilberforce Gosling vowed a vow that he would dismiss that distinguished novelist.

But the best intentions go for nothing when one's arm is feeling like lead. Of all the miserable balls sent down that afternoon that one of Gosling's was the worst. It was worse than anything of Marriott's. It flew sluggishly down the pitch well outside the leg stump. The novelist watched it come, and his eye gleamed. It was about to bounce for the second time when, with a pleased smile, the batsman stepped out. There was a loud, musical report, the note of a bat when it strikes the ball fairly on the driving spot.

The man of letters shaded his eyes with his hand, and watched the ball diminish in the distance.

'I rather think,' said he cheerfully, as a crash of glass told of its arrival at the Pavilion, 'that that does it.'

He was perfectly right. It did.

[9]

THE BISHOP FINISHES HIS RIDE

Gethryn had started on his ride handicapped by two things. He did not know his way after the first two miles, and the hedges at the roadside had just been clipped, leaving the roads covered with small thorns.

It was the former of these circumstances that first made itself apparent. For two miles the road ran straight, but after that it was unexplored country. The Bishop, being in both cricket and football teams, had few opportunities for cycling. He always brought his machine to School, but he very seldom used it.

At the beginning of the unexplored country, an irresponsible person recommended him to go straight on. He couldn't miss the road, said he. It was straight all the way. Gethryn thanked him, rode on, and having gone a mile came upon three roads, each of which might quite well have been considered a continuation of the road on which he was already. One curved gently off to the right, the other two equally gently to the left. He dismounted and the feelings of gratitude which he had borne towards his informant for his lucid directions vanished suddenly. He gazed searchingly at the three roads, but to single out one of them as straighter than the other two was a task that baffled him completely. A sign-post informed him of three things. By following road one he might get to Brindleham, and ultimately, if he persevered, to Corden. Road number two would lead him to Old Inns, whatever they might be, with the further inducement of Little Benbury, while if he cast in his lot with road three he might hope sooner or later to arrive at Much Middlefold-on-the-Hill, and Lesser Middlefold-in-the-Vale. But on the subject of Anfield and Anfield Junction the board was silent.

Two courses lay open to him. Should he select a route at random, or wait for somebody to come and direct him? He waited. He went on waiting. He waited a considerable time, and at last, just as he was about to trust to luck, and make for Much

49

Middlefold-on-the-Hill, a figure loomed in sight, a slow-moving man, who strolled down the Old Inns road at a pace which seemed to argue that he had plenty of time on his hands.

'I say, can you tell me the way to Anfield, please?' said the Bishop as he came up.

The man stopped, apparently rooted to the spot. He surveyed the Bishop with a glassy but determined stare from head to foot. Then he looked earnestly at the bicycle, and finally, in perfect silence, began to inspect the Bishop again.

'Eh?' he said at length.

'Can you tell me the way to Anfield?'

'Anfield?'

'Yes. How do I get there?'

The man perpended, and when he replied did so after the style of the late and great Ollendorf.

'Old Inns,' he said dreamily, waving a hand down the road by which he had come, 'be over there.'

'Yes, yes, I know,' said Gethryn.

'Was born at Old Inns, I was,' continued the man, warming to his subject. 'Lived there fifty-five years, I have. Yeou go straight down the road an' yeou cam t' Old Inns. Yes, that be the way t' Old Inns.'

Gethryn nobly refrained from rending the speaker limb from limb.

'I don't want to know the way to Old Inns,' he said desperately. 'Where I want to get is Anfield. Anfield, you know. Which way do I go?'

'Anfield?' said the man. Then a brilliant flash of intelligence illumined his countenance. 'Whoy, Anfield be same road as Old Inns. Yeou go straight down the road, an'—'

'Thanks very much,' said Gethryn, and without waiting for further revelations shot off in the direction indicated. A quarter of a mile farther he looked over his shoulder. The man was still there, gazing after him in a kind of trance.

The Bishop passed through Old Inns with some way on his machine. He had much lost time to make up. A signpost bearing the legend 'Anfield four miles' told him that he was nearing his destination. The notice had changed to three miles and again to two, when suddenly he felt that jarring sensation which every cyclist knows. His back tyre was punctured. It was impossible to ride on. He got off and walked. He was still in his cricket clothes, and the fact that he had on spiked boots did not make walking any the easier. His progress was not rapid.

Half an hour before his one wish had been to catch sight of a fellow-being. Now, when he would have preferred to have avoided his species, men seemed to spring up from nowhere, and every man of them had a remark to make or a question to ask about the punctured tyre. Reserve is not the leading characteristic of the average yokel.

Gethryn, however, refused to be drawn into conversation on the subject.

At last one, more determined than the rest, brought him to bay.

'Hoy, mister, stop,' called a voice. Gethryn turned. A man was running up the road towards him.

He arrived panting.

'What's up?' said the Bishop.

'You've got a puncture,' said the man, pointing an accusing finger at the flattened tyre.

It was not worth while killing the brute. Probably he was acting from the best motives.

'No,' said Gethryn wearily, 'it isn't a puncture. I always let the air out when I'm riding. It looks so much better, don't you think so? Why did they let you out? Good-bye.'

And feeling a little more comfortable after this outburst, he wheeled his bicycle on into Anfield High Street.

Minds in the village of Anfield worked with extraordinary rapidity. The first person of whom he asked the way to the Junction answered the riddle almost without thinking. He left his machine out in the road and went on to the platform. The first thing that caught his eye was the station clock with its hands pointing to five past four. And when he realized that, his uncle's train having left a clear half hour before, his labours had all been for nothing, the full bitterness of life came home to him.

He was turning away from the station when he stopped. Something else had caught his eye. On a bench at the extreme end of the platform sat a youth. And a further scrutiny convinced the Bishop of the fact that the youth was none other than Master Reginald Farnie, late of Beckford, and shortly, or he would know the reason why, to be once more of Beckford. Other people besides himself, it appeared, could miss trains.

Farnie was reading one of those halfpenny weeklies which—with a nerve which is the only creditable thing about them—call

51

themselves comic. He did not see the Bishop until a shadow falling across his paper caused him to look up.

It was not often that he found himself unequal to a situation. Monk in a recent conversation had taken him aback somewhat, but his feelings on that occasion were not to be compared with what he felt on seeing the one person whom he least desired to meet standing at his side. His jaw dropped limply, *Comic Blitherings* fluttered to the ground.

The Bishop was the first to speak. Indeed, if he had waited for Farnie to break the silence, he would have waited long.

'Get up,' he said. Farnie got up.

'Come on.' Farnie came.

'Go and get your machine,' said Gethryn. 'Hurry up. And now you will jolly well come back to Beckford, you little beast.'

But before that could be done there was Gethryn's back wheel to be mended. This took time. It was nearly half past four before they started.

'Oh,' said Gethryn, as they were about to mount, 'there's that money. I was forgetting. Out with it.'

Ten pounds had been the sum Farnie had taken from the study. Six was all he was able to restore. Gethryn enquired after the deficit.

'I gave it to Monk,' said Farnie.

To Gethryn, in his present frame of mind, the mere mention of Monk was sufficient to uncork the vials of his wrath.

'What the blazes did you do that for? What's Monk got to do with it?'

'He said he'd get me sacked if I didn't pay him,' whined Farnie.

This was not strictly true. Monk had not said. He had hinted. And he had hinted at flogging, not expulsion.

'Why?' pursued the Bishop. 'What had you and Monk been up to?'

Farnie, using his out-of-bounds adventures as a foundation, worked up a highly artistic narrative of doings, which, if they had actually been performed, would certainly have entailed expulsion. He had judged Gethryn's character correctly. If the matter had been simply a case for a flogging, the Bishop would have stood aside and let the thing go on. Against the extreme penalty of School law he felt bound as a matter of family duty to shield his relative. And he saw a bad time coming for himself in the very near future. Either he must expose Farnie, which he had resolved not to do, or he must refuse to explain his absence from the M.C.C. match, for by now there was not the smallest chance of his being able to get back in time for the visitors' innings. As he rode on he tried to imagine what would happen in consequence of that desertion, and he could not do it. His crime was, so far as he knew, absolutely without precedent in the School history.

As they passed the cricket field he saw that it was empty. Stumps were usually drawn early in the M.C.C. match if the issue of the game was out of doubt, as the Marylebone men had trains to catch. Evidently this had happened today. It might mean that the School had won easily—they had looked like making a big score when he had left the ground—in which case public opinion would be more lenient towards him. After a victory a school feels that all's well that ends well. But it might, on the other hand, mean quite the reverse.

He put his machine up, and hurried to the study. Several boys, as he passed them, looked curiously at him, but none spoke to him.

Marriott was in the study, reading a book. He was still in flannels, and looked as if he had begun to change but had thought better of it. As was actually the case.

'Hullo,' he cried, as Gethryn appeared. 'Where the dickens have you been all the afternoon? What on earth did you go off like that for?'

'I'm sorry, old chap,' said the Bishop, 'I can't tell you. I shan't be able to tell anyone.'

'But, man! Try and realize what you've done. Do you grasp the fact that you've gone and got the School licked in the M.C.C. match, and that we haven't beaten the M.C.C. for about a dozen years, and that if you'd been there to bowl we should have walked over this time? Do try and grasp the thing.'

'Did they win?'

'Rather. By a wicket. Two wickets, I mean. We made 213. Your bowling would just have done it.'

Gethryn sat down.

'Oh Lord,' he said blankly, 'this is awful!'

'But, look here, Bishop,' continued Marriott, 'this is all rot. You can't do a thing like this, and then refuse to offer any explanation, and expect things to go on just as usual.'

'I don't,' said Gethryn. 'I know there's going to be a row, but I can't explain. You'll have to take me on trust.'

'Oh, as far as I am concerned, it's all right,' said Marriott. 'I know you wouldn't be ass enough to do a thing like that without a jolly good reason. It's the other chaps I'm thinking about. You'll find it jolly hard to put Norris off, I'm afraid. He's most awfully sick about the match. He fielded badly, which always makes him shirty. Jephson, too. You'll have a bad time with Jephson. His one wish after the match was to have your gore and plenty of it. Nothing else would have pleased him a bit. And think of the chaps in the House, too. Just consider what a pull this gives Monk and his mob over you. The House'll want some looking after now, I fancy.'

'And they'll get it,' said Gethryn. 'If Monk gives me any of his beastly cheek, I'll knock his head off.'

But in spite of the consolation which such a prospect afforded him, he did not look forward with pleasure to the next day, when he would have to meet Norris and the rest. It would have been bad in any case. He did not care to think what would happen when he refused to offer the slightest explanation.

[10]

IN WHICH A CASE IS FULLY DISCUSSED

Gethryn was right in thinking that the interviews would be unpleasant. They increased in unpleasantness in arithmetical progression, until they culminated finally in a terrific encounter with the justly outraged Norris.

Reece was the first person to institute inquiries, and if everybody had resembled him, matters would not have been so bad for Gethryn. Reece possessed a perfect genius for minding his own business. The dialogue when they met was brief.

'Hullo,' said Reece.

'Hullo,' said the Bishop.

'Where did you get to yesterday?' said Reece.

'Oh, I had to go somewhere,' said the Bishop vaguely.

'Oh? Pity. Wasn't a bad match.' And that was all the comment Reece made on the situation.

Gethryn went over to the chapel that morning with an empty sinking feeling inside him. He was quite determined to offer no single word of explanation, and he felt that that made the prospect all the worse. There was a vast uncertainty in his mind as to what was going to happen. Nobody could actually do anything to him, of course. It would have been a decided relief to him if anybody had tried that line of action, for moments occur when the only thing that can adequately soothe the wounded spirit, is to hit straight from the shoulder at someone. The punching-ball is often found useful under these circumstances. As he was passing Jephson's House he nearly ran into somebody who was coming out.

'Be firm, my moral pecker,' thought Gethryn, and braced himself up for conflict.

'Well, Gethryn?' said Mr Jephson.

The question 'Well?' especially when addressed by a master to a boy, is one of the few questions to which there is literally no answer. You can look sheepish, you can look defiant, or you can look surprised according to the state of your conscience. But anything in the way of verbal response is impossible.

Gethryn attempted no verbal response.

'Well, Gethryn,' went on Mr Jephson, 'was it pleasant up the river yesterday?'

Mr Jephson always preferred the rapier of sarcasm to the bludgeon of abuse.

'Yes, sir,' said Gethryn, 'very pleasant.' He did not mean to be massacred without a struggle.

'What!' cried Mr Jephson. 'You actually mean to say that you did go up the river?'

'No, sir.'

'Then what do you mean?'

'It is always pleasant up the river on a fine day,' said Gethryn.

His opponent, to use a metaphor suitable to a cricket master, changed his action. He abandoned sarcasm and condescended to direct inquiry.

'Where were you yesterday afternoon?' he said.

The Bishop, like Mr Hurry Bungsho Jabberjee, B.A., became at once the silent tomb.

'Did you hear what I said, Gethryn?' (icily). 'Where were you yesterday afternoon?'

'I can't say, sir.'

These words may convey two meanings. They may imply ignorance, in which case the speaker should be led gently off to the nearest asylum. Or they may imply obstinacy. Mr Jephson decided that in the present case obstinacy lay at the root of the matter. He became icier than ever.

'Very well, Gethryn,' he said, 'I shall report this to the Headmaster.'

And Gethryn, feeling that the conference was at an end, proceeded on his way.

After chapel there was Norris to be handled. Norris had been rather late for chapel that morning, and had no opportunity of speaking to the Bishop. But after the service was over, and the School streamed out of the building towards their respective houses, he waylaid him at the door, and demanded an explanation. The Bishop refused to give one. Norris, whose temper never had a chance of reaching its accustomed tranquillity until he had consumed some breakfast—he hated early morning chapel—raved. The Bishop was worried, but firm.

'Then you mean to say—you don't mean to say—I mean, you don't intend to explain?' said Norris finally, working round for the twentieth time to his original text.

'I can't explain.'

'You won't, you mean.'

'Yes. I'll apologize if you like, but I won't explain.'

Norris felt the strain was becoming too much for him.

'Apologize!' he moaned, addressing circumambient space. 'Apologize! A man cuts off in the middle of the M.C.C. match, loses us the game, and then comes back and offers to apologize.'

'The offer's withdrawn,' put in Gethryn. 'Apologies and explanations are both off.' It was hopeless to try and be conciliatory under the circumstances. They did not admit of it.

Norris glared.

'I suppose,' he said, 'you don't expect to go on playing for the First after this? We can't keep a place open for you in the team on the off chance of your not having a previous engagement, you know.'

'That's your affair,' said the Bishop, 'you're captain. Have you finished your address? Is there anything else you'd like to say?'

Norris considered, and, as he went in at Jephson's gate, wound up with this Parthian shaft—

'All I can say is that you're not fit to be at a public school. They ought to sack a chap for doing that sort of thing. If you'll take my advice, you'll leave.'

About two hours afterwards Gethryn discovered a suitable retort, but, coming to the conclusion that better late than never does not apply to repartees, refrained from speaking it.

It was Mr Jephson's usual custom to sally out after supper on Sunday evenings to smoke a pipe (or several pipes) with one of the other House-masters. On this particular evening he made for Robertson's, which was one of the four Houses on the opposite side of the School grounds. He could hardly have selected a better man to take his grievance to. Mr Robertson was a long, silent man with grizzled hair, and an eye that pierced like a gimlet. He had the enviable reputation of keeping the best order of any master in the School. He was also one of the most popular of the staff. This was all the more remarkable from the fact that he played no games.

To him came Mr Jephson, primed to bursting point with his grievance.

'Anything wrong, Jephson?' said Mr Robertson.

'Wrong? I should just think there was. Did you happen to be looking at the match yesterday, Robertson?'

Mr Robertson nodded.

'I always watch School matches. Good match. Norris missed a bad catch in the slips. He was asleep.'

Mr Jephson conceded the point. It was trivial.

'Yes,' he said, 'he should certainly have held it. But that's a mere detail. I want to talk about Gethryn. Do you know what he did yesterday? I never heard of such a thing in my life, never. Went off during the luncheon interval without a word, and never appeared again till lock-up. And now he refuses to offer any explanation whatever. I shall report the whole thing to Beckett. I told Gethryn so this morning.'

'I shouldn't,' said Mr Robertson; 'I really think I shouldn't. Beckett finds the ordinary duties of a Headmaster quite sufficient for his needs. This business is not in his province at all.'

'Not in his province? My dear sir, what is a headmaster for, if not to manage affairs of this sort?'

Mr Robertson smiled in a sphinx-like manner, and answered, after the fashion of Socrates, with a question.

'Let me ask you two things, Jephson. You must proceed gingerly. Now, firstly, it is a headmaster's business to punish any breach of school rules, is it not?'

'Well?'

'And school prefects do not attend roll-call, and have no restrictions placed upon them in the matter of bounds?'

'No. Well?'

'Then perhaps you'll tell me what School rule Gethryn has broken?' said

Mr Robertson.

'You see you can't,' he went on. 'Of course you can't. He has not broken any School rule. He is a prefect, and may do anything he likes with his spare time. He chooses to play cricket. Then he changes his mind and goes off to some unknown locality for some reason at present unexplained. It is all perfectly legal. Extremely quaint behaviour on his part, I admit, but thoroughly legal.'

'Then nothing can be done,' exclaimed Mr Jephson blankly. 'But it's absurd. Something must be done. The thing can't be left as it is. It's preposterous!'

'I should imagine,' said Mr Robertson, 'from what small knowledge I possess of the Human Boy, that matters will be made decidedly unpleasant for the criminal.'

'Well, I know one thing; he won't play for the team again.'

'There is something very refreshing about your logic, Jephson. Because a boy does not play in one match, you will not let him play in any of the others, though you admit his absence weakens the team. However, I suppose that is unavoidable. Mind you, I think it is a pity. Of course Gethryn has some explanation, if he would only favour us with it. Personally I think rather highly of Gethryn. So does poor old Leicester. He is the only Head-prefect Leicester has had for the last half-dozen years who knows even the rudiments of his business. But it's no use my preaching his virtues to you. You wouldn't listen. Take another cigar, and let's talk about the weather.'

Mr Jephson took the proffered weed, and the conversation, though it did not turn upon the suggested topic, ceased to have anything to do with Gethryn.

The general opinion of the School was dead against the Bishop. One or two of his friends still clung to a hope that explanations might come out, while there were also a few who always made a point of thinking differently from everybody else. Of this class was Pringle. On the Monday after the match he spent the best part of an hour of his valuable time reasoning on the subject with Lorimer. Lorimer's vote went with the majority. Although he had fielded for the Bishop, he was not, of course, being merely a substitute, allowed to bowl, as the Bishop had had his innings, and it had been particularly galling to him to feel that he might have saved the match, if it had only been possible for him to have played a larger part.

'It's no good jawing about it,' he said, 'there isn't a word to say for the man. He hasn't a leg to stand on. Why, it would be bad enough in a House or form match even, but when it comes to first matches—!' Here words failed Lorimer.

'Not at all,' said Pringle, unmoved. 'There are heaps of reasons, jolly good reasons, why he might have gone away.'

'Such as?' said Lorimer.

'Well, he might have been called away by a telegram, for instance.'

'What rot! Why should he make such a mystery of it if that was all?'

'He'd have explained all right if somebody had asked him properly. You get a chap like Norris, who, when he loses his hair, has got just about as much tact as a rhinoceros, going and ballyragging the man, and no wonder he won't say anything. I shouldn't myself.'

'Well, go and talk to him decently, then. Let's see you do it, and I'll bet it won't make a bit of difference. What the chap has done is to go and get himself mixed up in some shady business somewhere. That's the only thing it can be.'

'Rot,' said Pringle, 'the Bishop isn't that sort of chap.'

'You can't tell. I say,' he broke off suddenly, 'have you done that poem yet?'

Pringle started. He had not so much as begun that promised epic.

'I—er—haven't quite finished it yet. I'm thinking it out, you know.

Getting a sort of general grip of the thing.'

'Oh. Well, I wish you'd buck up with it. It's got to go in tomorrow week.'

'Tomorrow week. Tuesday the what? Twenty-second, isn't it? Right. I'll

remember. Two days after the O.B.s' match. That'll fix it in my mind.

By the way, your people are going to come down all right, aren't they?

I mean, we shall have to be getting in supplies and so on.'

'Yes. They'll be coming. There's plenty of time, though, to think of that. What you've got to do for the present is to keep your mind glued on the death of Dido.'

'Rather,' said Pringle, 'I won't forget.'

This was at six twenty-two p.m. By the time six-thirty boomed from the College clock-tower, Pringle was absorbing a thrilling work of fiction, and Dido, her death, and everything connected with her, had faded from his mind like a beautiful dream.

[11]

POETRY AND STUMP-CRICKET

The Old Beckfordians' match came off in due season, and Pringle enjoyed it thoroughly. Though he only contributed a dozen in the first innings, he made up for this afterwards in the second, when the School had a hundred and twenty to get in just two hours. He went in first with Marriott, and they pulled the thing off and gave the School a ten wickets victory with eight minutes to spare. Pringle was in rare form. He made fifty-three, mainly off the bowling of a certain J.R. Smith, whose fag he had been in the old days. When at School, Smith had always been singularly aggressive towards Pringle, and the latter found that much pleasure was to be derived from hitting fours off his bowling. Subsequently he ate more strawberries and cream than were, strictly speaking, good for him, and did the honours at the study tea-party with the grace of a born host. And, as he had hoped, Miss Mabel Lorimer *did* ask what that silver-plate was stuck on to that bat for.

It is not to be wondered at that in the midst of these festivities such trivialities as Lorimer's poem found no place in his thoughts. It was not until the following day that he was reminded of it.

That Sunday was a visiting Sunday. Visiting Sundays occurred three times a term, when everybody who had friends and relations in the neighbourhood was allowed to spend the day with them. Pringle on such occasions used to ride over to Biddlehampton, the scene of Farnie's adventures, on somebody else's bicycle, his destination being the residence of a certain Colonel Ashby, no relation, but a great friend of his father's.

The gallant Colonel had, besides his other merits—which were numerous—the pleasant characteristic of leaving his guests to themselves. To be left to oneself under some circumstances is apt to be a drawback, but in this case there was never any lack of amusements. The only objection that Pringle ever found was that there was too much to do in the time. There was shooting, riding, fishing, and also stump-cricket. Given proper conditions, no game in existence yields to stump-cricket in the matter of excitement. A stable-yard makes the best pitch, for the walls stop all hits and you score solely by boundaries, one for every hit, two if it goes past the coach-room door, four to the end wall, and out if you send it over. It is perfect.

There were two junior Ashbys, twins, aged sixteen. They went to school at Charchester, returning to the ancestral home for the weekend. Sometimes when Pringle came they would bring a school friend, in which case Pringle and he would play the twins. But as a rule the programme consisted of a series of five test matches, Charchester *versus* Beckford; and as Pringle was almost exactly twice as good as each of the twins taken individually, when they combined it made the sides very even, and the test matches were fought out with the most deadly keenness.

After lunch the Colonel was in the habit of taking Pringle for a stroll in the grounds, to watch him smoke a cigar or two. On this Sunday the conversation during the walk, after beginning, as was right and proper, with cricket, turned to work.

'Let me see,' said the Colonel, as Pringle finished the description of how point had almost got to the square cut which had given him his century against Charchester, 'you're out of the Upper Fifth now, aren't you? I always used to think you were going to be a fixture there. You are like your father in that way. I remember him at Rugby spending years on end in the same form. Couldn't get out of it. But you did get your remove, if I remember?'

'Rather,' said Pringle, 'years ago. That's to say, last term. And I'm jolly glad I did, too.'

His errant memory had returned to the poetry prize once more.

'Oh,' said the Colonel, 'why is that?'

Pringle explained the peculiar disadvantages that attended membership of the Upper Fifth during the summer term.

'I don't think a man ought to be allowed to spend his money in these special prizes,' he concluded; 'at any rate they ought to be Sixth Form affairs. It's hard enough having to do the ordinary work and keep up your cricket at the same time.'

'They are compulsory then?'

'Yes. Swindle, I call it. The chap who shares my study at Beckford is in the Upper Fifth, and his hair's turning white under the strain. The worst of it is, too, that I've promised to help him, and I never seem to have any time to give to the thing. I could turn out a great poem if I had an hour or two to spare now and then.'

'What's the subject?'

'Death of Dido this year. They are always jolly keen on deaths. Last year it was Cato, and the year before Julius Caesar. They seem to have very morbid minds. I think they might try something cheerful for a change.'

'Dido,' said the Colonel dreamily. 'Death of Dido. Where have I heard either a story or a poem or a riddle or something in some way connected with the death of Dido? It was years ago, but I

61

distinctly remember having heard somebody mention the occurrence. Oh, well, it will come back presently, I dare say.'

It did come back presently. The story was this. A friend of Colonel Ashby's—the one-time colonel of his regiment, to be exact—was an earnest student of everything in the literature of the country that dealt with Sport. This gentleman happened to read in a publisher's list one day that a limited edition of *The Dark Horse*, by a Mr Arthur James, was on sale, and might be purchased from the publisher by all who were willing to spend half a guinea to that end.

'Well, old Matthews,' said the Colonel, 'sent off for this book. Thought it must be a sporting novel, don't you know. I shall never forget his disappointment when he opened the parcel. It turned out to be a collection of poems. *The Dark Horse, and Other Studies in the Tragic*, was its full title.'

'Matthews never had a soul for poetry, good or bad. *The Dark Horse* itself was about a knight in the Middle Ages, you know. Great nonsense it was, too. Matthews used to read me passages from time to time. When he gave up the regiment he left me the book as a farewell gift. He said I was the only man he knew who really sympathized with him in the affair. I've got it still. It's in the library somewhere, if you care to look at it. What recalled it to my mind was your mention of Dido. The second poem was about the death of Dido, as far as I can remember. I'm no judge of poetry, but it didn't strike me as being very good. At the same time, you might pick up a hint or two from it. It ought to be in one of the two lower shelves on the right of the door as you go in. Unless it has been taken away. That is not likely, though. We are not very enthusiastic poetry readers here.'

Pringle thanked him for his information, and went back to the stable-yard, where he lost the fourth test match by sixteen runs, owing to preoccupation. You can't play a yorker on the leg-stump with a thin walking-stick if your mind is occupied elsewhere. And the leg-stump yorkers of James, the elder (by a minute) of the two Ashbys, were achieving a growing reputation in Charchester cricket circles.

One ought never, thought Pringle, to despise the gifts which Fortune bestows on us. And this mention of an actual completed poem on the very subject which was in his mind was clearly a gift of Fortune. How much better it would be to read thoughtfully through this poem, and quarry out a set of verses from it suitable to Lorimer's needs, than to waste his brain-tissues in trying to evolve something original from his own inner consciousness.

Pringle objected strongly to any unnecessary waste of his brain-tissues. Besides, the best poets borrowed. Virgil did it. Tennyson did it. Even Homer—we have it on the authority of Mr Kipling—when he smote his blooming lyre went and stole what he thought he might require. Why should Pringle of the School House refuse to follow in such illustrious footsteps?

It was at this point that the guileful James delivered his insidious yorker, and the dull thud of the tennis ball on the board which served as the wicket told a listening world that Charchester had won the fourth test match, and that the scores were now two all.

But Beckford's star was to ascend again. Pringle's mind was made up. He would read the printed poem that very night, and before retiring to rest he would have Lorimer's verses complete and ready to be sent in for judgement to the examiner. But for the present he would dismiss the matter from his mind, and devote himself to polishing off the Charchester champions in the fifth and final test match. And in this he was successful, for just as the bell rang, summoning the players in to a well-earned tea, a sweet forward drive from his walking-stick crashed against the end wall, and Beckford had won the rubber.

'As the young batsman, undefeated to the last, reached the pavilion,' said Pringle, getting into his coat, 'a prolonged and deafening salvo of cheers greeted him. His twenty-three not out, compiled as it was against the finest bowling Charchester could produce, and on a wicket that was always treacherous (there's a brick loose at the top end), was an effort unique in its heroism.'

'Oh, *come* on,' said the defeated team.

'If you have fluked a win,' said James, 'it's nothing much. Wait till next visiting Sunday.'

And the teams went in to tea.

In the programme which Pringle had mapped out for himself, he was to go to bed with his book at the highly respectable hour of ten, work till eleven, and then go to sleep. But programmes are notoriously subject to alterations. Pringle's was altered owing to a remark made immediately after dinner by John Ashby, who, desirous of retrieving the fallen fortunes of Charchester, offered to play Pringle a hundred up at billiards, giving him thirty. Now Pringle's ability in the realm of sport did not extend to billiards. But the human being who can hear unmoved a fellow human being offering him thirty start in a game of a hundred has yet to be born. He accepted the challenge, and permission to play having been granted by the powers that were, on the understanding that the cloth was not to be cut and as few cues broken as possible, the game began, James acting as marker.

There are doubtless ways by which a game of a hundred up can be got through in less than two hours, but with Pringle and his opponent desire outran performance. When the highest break on either side is six, and the average break two, matters progress with more stateliness than speed. At last, when the hands of the clock both pointed to the figure eleven, Pringle, whose score had been at ninety-eight since half-past ten, found himself within two inches of his opponent's ball, which was tottering on the very edge of the pocket. He administered the *coup de grace* with the air of a John Roberts, and retired triumphant; while the Charchester representatives pointed out that as their score was at seventy-four, they had really won a moral victory by four points. To which specious and unsportsmanlike piece of sophistry Pringle turned a deaf ear.

It was now too late for any serious literary efforts. No bard can do without his sleep. Even Homer used to nod at times. So Pringle contented himself with reading through the poem, which consisted of some thirty lines, and copying the same down on a sheet of notepaper for future reference. After which he went to bed.

In order to arrive at Beckford in time for morning school, he had to start from the house at eight o'clock punctually. This left little time for poetical lights. The consequence was that when Lorimer, on the following afternoon, demanded the poem as per contract, all that Pringle had to show was the copy which he had made of the poem in the book. There was a moment's suspense while Conscience and Sheer Wickedness fought the matter out inside him, and then Conscience, which had started on the encounter without enthusiasm, being obviously flabby and out of condition, threw up the sponge.

'Here you are,' said Pringle, 'it's only a rough copy, but here it *is*.'

Lorimer perused it hastily.

'But, I say,' he observed in surprised and awestruck tones, 'this is rather good.'

It seemed to strike him as quite a novel idea. 'Yes, not bad, is it?'

'But it'll get the prize.'

'Oh, we shall have to prevent that somehow.'

He did not mention how, and Lorimer did not ask.

'Well, anyhow,' said Lorimer, 'thanks awfully. I hope you've not fagged about it too much.'

'Oh no,' said Pringle airily, 'rather not. It's been no trouble at all.'

He thus, it will be noticed, concluded a painful and immoral scene by speaking perfect truth. A most gratifying reflection.

[12]

'WE, THE UNDERSIGNED—'

Norris kept his word with regard to the Bishop's exclusion from the Eleven. The team which had beaten the O.B.s had not had the benefit of his assistance, Lorimer appearing in his stead. Lorimer was a fast right-hand bowler, deadly in House matches or on a very bad wicket. He was the mainstay of the Second Eleven attack, and in an ordinary year would have been certain of his First Eleven cap. This season, however, with Gosling, Baynes, and the Bishop, the School had been unusually strong, and Lorimer had had to wait.

The non-appearance of his name on the notice-board came as no surprise to Gethryn. He had had the advantage of listening to Norris's views on the subject. But when Marriott grasped the facts of the case, he went to Norris and raved. Norris, as is right and proper in the captain of a School team when the wisdom of his actions is called into question, treated him with no respect whatever.

'It's no good talking,' he said, when Marriott had finished a brisk opening speech, 'I know perfectly well what I'm doing.'

'Then there's no excuse for you at all,' said Marriott. 'If you were mad or delirious I could understand it.'

'Come and have an ice,' said Norris.

'Ice!' snorted Marriott. 'What's the good of standing there babbling about ices! Do you know we haven't beaten the O.B.s for four years?'

'We shall beat them this year.'

'Not without Gethryn.'

'We certainly shan't beat them with Gethryn, because he's not going to play. A chap who chooses the day of the M.C.C. match to go off for the afternoon, and then refuses to explain, can consider himself jolly well chucked until further notice. Feel ready for that ice yet?'

'Don't be an ass.'

'Well, if ever you do get any ice, take my tip and tie it carefully round your head in a handkerchief. Then perhaps you'll be able to see why Gethryn isn't playing against the O.B.s on Saturday.'

And Marriott went off raging, and did not recover until late in the afternoon, when he made eighty-three in an hour for Leicester's House in a scratch game.

There were only three of the eleven Houses whose occupants seriously expected to see the House cricket cup on the mantelpiece of their dining-room at the end of the season. These were the School House, Jephson's, and Leicester's. In view of Pringle's sensational feats throughout the term, the knowing ones thought that the cup would go to the School House, with Leicester's runners-up. The various members of the First Eleven were pretty evenly distributed throughout the three Houses. Leicester's had Gethryn, Reece, and Marriott. Jephson's relied on Norris, Bruce, and Baker. The School House trump card was Pringle, with Lorimer and Baynes to do the bowling, and Hill of the First Eleven and Kynaston and Langdale of the second to back him up in the batting department. Both the other First Eleven men were day boys.

The presence of Gosling in any of the House elevens, however weak on paper, would have lent additional interest to the fight for the cup; for in House matches, where every team has more or less of a tail, one really good fast bowler can make a surprising amount of difference to a side.

There was a great deal of interest in the School about the House cup. The keenest of all games at big schools are generally the House matches. When Beckford met Charchester or any of the four schools which it played at cricket and football, keenness reached its highest pitch. But next to these came the House matches.

Now that he no longer played for the Eleven, the Bishop was able to give his whole mind to training the House team in the way it should go. Exclusion from the First Eleven meant also that he could no longer, unless possessed of an amount of *sang-froid* so colossal as almost to amount to genius, put in an appearance at the First Eleven net. Under these circumstances Leicester's net summoned him. Like Mr Phil May's lady when she was ejected (with perfect justice) by a barman, he went somewhere where he would be respected. To the House, then, he devoted himself, and scratch games and before-breakfast field-outs became the order of the day.

House fielding before breakfast is one of the things which cannot be classed under the head of the Lighter Side of Cricket. You get up in the small hours, dragged from a comfortable bed by some sportsman who, you feel, carries enthusiasm to a point where it ceases to be a virtue and becomes a nuisance. You get into flannels, and, still half asleep, stagger off to the field, where a hired ruffian hits you up catches which bite like serpents and sting like adders. From time to time he adds insult to injury by shouting 'get to 'em!', 'get to 'em!'—a remark which finds but one parallel in the language, the 'keep moving' of the football captain. Altogether there are many more pleasant occupations than early morning field-outs, and it requires a considerable amount of keenness to carry the victim through them without hopelessly souring his nature and causing him to foster uncharitable thoughts towards his House captain.

J. Monk of Leicester's found this increased activity decidedly uncongenial. He had no real patriotism in him. He played cricket well, but he played entirely for himself.

If, for instance, he happened to make fifty in a match—and it happened fairly frequently—he vastly preferred that the rest of the side should make ten between them than that there should be any more half-centuries on the score sheet, even at the expense of losing the match. It was not likely, therefore, that he would take kindly to this mortification of the flesh, the sole object of which was to make everybody as conspicuous as everybody else. Besides, in the matter of fielding he considered that he had nothing to learn, which, as Euclid would say, was absurd. Fielding is one of the things which is never perfect.

Monk, moreover, had another reason for disliking the field-outs. Gethryn, as captain of the House team, was naturally master of the ceremonies, and Monk objected to Gethryn. For this dislike he had solid reasons. About a fortnight after the commencement of term, the Bishop, going downstairs from his study one afternoon, was aware of what appeared to be a species of free fight going on in the doorway of the senior day-room. The senior day-room was where the rowdy element of the House collected, the individuals who were too old to be fags, and too low down in the School to own studies.

Under ordinary circumstances the Bishop would probably have passed on without investigating the matter. A head of a house hates above all things to get a name for not minding his own business in unimportant matters. Such a reputation tells against him when he has to put his foot down over big things. To have invaded the senior day-room and stopped a conventional senior day-room 'rag' would have been interfering with the most cherished rights of the citizens, the freedom which is the birthright of every Englishman, so to speak.

But as he passed the door which had just shut with a bang behind the free fighters, he heard Monk's voice inside, and immediately afterwards the voice of Danvers, and he stopped. In the first place, he reasoned within himself, if Monk and Danvers were doing anything, it was probably something wrong, and ought to be stopped. Gethryn always had the feeling that it was his duty to go and see what Monk and Danvers were doing, and tell them they mustn't. He had a profound belief in their irreclaimable villainy. In the second place, having studies of their own, they had no business to be in the senior day-room at all. It was contrary to the etiquette of the House for a study man to enter the senior day-room, and as a rule the senior day-room resented it. As to all appearances they were not resenting it now, the obvious conclusion was that something was going on which ought to cease.

The Bishop opened the door. Etiquette did not compel the head of the House to knock, the rule being that you knocked only at the doors of those senior to you in the House. He was consequently enabled to witness a tableau which, if warning had been received of his coming, would possibly have broken up before he entered. In the centre of the group was Wilson, leaning over the study table, not so much as if he liked so leaning as because he was held in that position by Danvers. In the background stood Monk, armed with a walking-stick. Round the walls were various ornaments of the senior day-room in attitudes of expectant attention, being evidently content to play the part of 'friends and retainers', leaving the leading parts in the hands of Monk and his colleague.

'Hullo,' said the Bishop, 'what's going on?'

'It's all right, old chap,' said Monk, grinning genially, 'we're only having an execution.'

'What's the row?' said the Bishop. 'What's Wilson been doing?'

'Nothing,' broke in that youth, who had wriggled free from Danvers's clutches. 'I haven't done a thing, Gethryn. These beasts lugged me out of the junior day-room without saying what for or anything.'

The Bishop began to look dangerous. This had all the outward aspect of a case of bullying. Under Reynolds's leadership

68

Leicester's had gone in rather extensively for bullying, and the Bishop had waited hungrily for a chance of catching somebody actively engaged in the sport, so that he might drop heavily on that person and make life unpleasant for him.

'Well?' he said, turning to Monk, 'let's have it. What was it all about, and what have you got to do with it?'

Monk began to shuffle.

'Oh, it was nothing much,' he said.

'Then what are you doing with the stick?' pursued the Bishop relentlessly.

'Young Wilson cheeked Perkins,' said Monk.

Murmurs of approval from the senior day-room. Perkins was one of the ornaments referred to above.

'How?' asked Gethryn.

Wilson dashed into the conversation again.

'Perkins told me to go and get him some grub from the shop. I was doing some work, so I couldn't. Besides, I'm not his fag. If Perkins wants to go for me, why doesn't he do it himself, and not get about a hundred fellows to help him?'

'Exactly,' said the Bishop. 'A very sensible suggestion. Perkins, fall upon Wilson and slay him. I'll see fair play. Go ahead.'

'Er—no,' said Perkins uneasily. He was a small, weedy-looking youth, not built for fighting except by proxy, and he remembered the episode of Wilson and Skinner.

'Then the thing's finished,' said Gethryn. 'Wilson walks over. We needn't detain you, Wilson.'

Wilson departed with all the honours of war, and the Bishop turned to

Monk.

'Now perhaps you'll tell me,' he said, 'what the deuce you and Danvers are doing here?'

'Well, hang it all, old chap—'

The Bishop begged that Monk would not call him 'old chap'.

'I'll call you "sir", if you like,' said Monk.

A gleam of hope appeared in the Bishop's eye. Monk was going to give him the opportunity he had long sighed for. In cold blood he could attack no one, not even Monk, but if he was going to be rude, that altered matters.

'What business have you in the day-room?' he said. 'You've got studies of your own.'

'If it comes to that,' said Monk, 'so have you. We've got as much business here as you. What the deuce are you doing here?'

Taken by itself, taken neat, as it were, this repartee might have been insufficient to act as a *casus belli*, but by a merciful dispensation of Providence the senior day-room elected to laugh at the remark, and to laugh loudly. Monk also laughed. Not, however, for long. The next moment the Bishop had darted in, knocked his feet from under him, and dragged him to the door. Captain Kettle himself could not have done it more neatly.

'Now,' said the Bishop, 'we can discuss the point.'

Monk got up, looking greener than usual, and began to dust his clothes.

'Don't talk rot,' he said, 'I can't fight a prefect.'

This, of course, the Bishop had known all along. What he had intended to do if Monk had kept up his end he had not decided when he embarked upon the engagement. The head of a House cannot fight by-battles with his inferiors without the loss of a good deal of his painfully acquired dignity. But Gethryn knew Monk, and he had felt justified in risking it. He improved the shining hour with an excursus on the subject of bullying, dispensed a few general threats, and left the room.

Monk had—perhaps not unnaturally—not forgotten the incident, and now that public opinion ran strongly against Gethryn on account of his M.C.C. match manoeuvres, he acted. A mass meeting of the Mob was called in his study, and it was unanimously voted that field-outs in the morning were undesirable, and that it would be judicious if the team were to strike. Now, as the Mob included in their numbers eight of the House Eleven, their opinions on the subject carried weight.

'Look here,' said Waterford, struck with a brilliant idea, 'I tell you what we'll do. Let's sign a round-robin refusing to play in the House matches unless Gethryn resigns the captaincy and the field-outs stop.'

'We may as well sign in alphabetical order,' said Monk prudently.

'It'll make it safer.'

The idea took the Mob's fancy. The round-robin was drawn up and signed.

'Now, if we could only get Reece,' suggested Danvers. 'It's no good asking Marriott, but Reece might sign.'

'Let's have a shot at any rate,' said Monk.

And a deputation, consisting of Danvers, Waterford, and Monk, duly waited upon Reece in his study, and broached the project to him.

LEICESTER'S HOUSE TEAM GOES INTO A SECOND EDITION

Reece was working when the deputation entered. He looked up enquiringly, but if he was pleased to see his visitors he managed to conceal the fact.

'Oh, I say, Reece,' began Monk, who had constituted himself spokesman to the expedition, 'are you busy?'

'Yes,' said Reece simply, going on with his writing.

This might have discouraged some people, but Nature had equipped Monk with a tough skin, which hints never pierced. He dropped into a chair, crossed his legs, and coughed. Danvers and Waterford leaned in picturesque attitudes against the door and mantelpiece. There was a silence for a minute, during which Reece continued to write unmoved.

'Take a seat, Monk,' he said at last, without looking up.

'Oh, er, thanks, I have,' said Monk. 'I say, Reece, we wanted to speak to you.'

'Go ahead then,' said Reece. 'I can listen and write at the same time.

I'm doing this prose against time.'

'It's about Gethryn.'

'What's Gethryn been doing?'

'Oh, I don't know. Nothing special. It's about his being captain of the

House team. The chaps seem to think he ought to resign.'

'Which chaps?' enquired Reece, laying down his pen and turning round in his chair.

'The rest of the team, you know.'

'Why don't they think he ought to be captain? The head of the House is always captain of the House team unless he's too bad to be in it at all. Don't the chaps think Gethryn's good at cricket?'

'Oh, he's good enough,' said Monk. 'It's more about this M.C.C. match business, you know. His cutting off like that in the middle of the match. The chaps think the House ought to take some notice of it. Express its disapproval, and that sort of thing.'

'And what do the chaps think of doing about it?'

Monk inserted a hand in his breast-pocket, and drew forth the round-robin. He straightened it out, and passed it over to Reece.

'We've drawn up this notice,' he said, 'and we came to see if you'd sign it. Nearly all the other chaps in the team have.'

Reece perused the document gravely. Then he handed it back to its owner.

'What rot,' said he.

'I don't think so at all,' said Monk.

'Nor do I,' broke in Danvers, speaking for the first time. 'What else can we do? We can't let a chap like Gethryn stick to the captaincy.'

'Why not?'

'A cad like that!'

'That's a matter of opinion. I don't suppose everyone thinks him a cad.

I don't, personally.'

'Well, anyway,' asked Waterford, 'are you going to sign?'

'My good man, of course I'm not. Do you mean to say you seriously intend to hand in that piffle to Gethryn?'

'Rather,' said Monk.

'Then you'll be making fools of yourselves. I'll tell you exactly what'll happen, if you care to know. Gethryn will read this rot, and simply cut everybody whose name appears on the list out of the House team. I don't know if you're aware of it, but there are several other fellows besides you in the House. And if you come to think of it, you aren't so awfully good. You three are in the Second. The other five haven't got colours at all.'

'Anyhow, we're all in the House team,' said Monk.

'Don't let that worry you,' said Reece, 'you won't be long, if you show

Gethryn that interesting document. Anything else I can do for you?'

'No, thanks,' said Monk. And the deputation retired.

When they had gone, Reece made his way to the Bishop's study. It was not likely that the deputation would deliver their ultimatum until late at night, when the study would be empty. From what Reece knew of Monk, he judged that it would be pleasanter to him to leave the document where the Bishop could find it in the morning, rather than run the risks that might attend a personal interview. There was time, therefore, to let Gethryn know what was going to happen, so that he might not be surprised into doing anything rash, such as resigning the captaincy, for example. Not that Reece thought it likely that he would, but it was better to take no risks.

Both Marriott and Gethryn were in the study when he arrived.

'Hullo, Reece,' said Marriott, 'come in and take several seats. Have
 a biscuit? Have two. Have a good many.'

Reece helped himself, and gave them a brief description of the late interview.

'I'm not surprised,' said Gethryn, 'I thought Monk would be getting at me somehow soon. I shall *have* to slay that chap someday. What ought I to do, do you think?'

'My dear chap,' said Marriott, 'there's only one thing you can do. Cut the lot of them out of the team, and fill up with substitutes.'

Reece nodded approval.

'Of course. That's what you must do. As a matter of fact, I told them you would. I've given you a reputation. You must live up to it.'

'Besides,' continued Marriott, 'after all it isn't such a crusher, when you come to think of it. Only four of them are really certainties for their places, Monk, Danvers, Waterford, and Saunders. The rest are simply tail.'

Reece nodded again. 'Great minds think alike. Exactly what I told them, only they wouldn't listen.'

'Well, whom do you suggest instead of them? Some of the kids are jolly keen and all that, but they wouldn't be much good against Baynes and Lorimer, for instance.'

'If I were you,' said Marriott, 'I shouldn't think about their batting at all. I should go simply for fielding. With a good fielding side we ought to have quite a decent chance. There's no earthly reason why you and Reece shouldn't put on enough for the first wicket to win all the matches. It's been done before. Don't you remember the School House getting the cup four years ago when Twiss was captain? They had nobody who was any earthly good except Twiss and Birch, and those two used to make about a hundred and fifty between them in every match. Besides, some of the kids can bat rather well. Wilson for one. He can bowl, too.'

'Yes,' said the Bishop, 'all right. Stick down Wilson. Who else? Gregson isn't bad. He can field in the slips, which is more than a good many chaps can.'

'Gregson's good,' said Reece, 'put him down. That makes five. You might have young Lee in too. I've seen him play like a book at his form net once or twice.'

'Lee—six. Five more wanted. Where's a House list? Here we are. Now. Adams, Bond, Brown, Burgess. Burgess has his points. Shall I stick him down?'

'Not presume to dictate,' said Marriott, 'but Adams is streets better than Burgess as a field, and just as good a bat.'

'Why, when have you seen him?'

'In a scratch game between his form and another. He was carting all over the shop. Made thirty something.'

'We'll have both of them in, then. Plenty of room. This is the team so far. Wilson, Gregson, Lee, Adams, and Burgess, with Marriott, Reece, and Gethryn. Jolly hot stuff it is, too, by Jove. We'll simply walk that tankard. Now, for the last places. I vote we each select a man, and nobody's allowed to appeal against the other's decision. I lead off with Crowinshaw. Good name, Crowinshaw. Look well on a score sheet.'

'Heave us the list,' said Marriott. 'Thanks. My dear sir, there's only one man in the running at all, which his name's Chamberlain. Shove down Joseph, and don't let me hear anyone breathe a word against him. Come on, Reece, let's have your man. I bet Reece selects some weird rotter.'

Reece pondered.

'Carstairs,' he said.

'Oh, my very dear sir! Carstairs!'

'All criticism barred,' said the Bishop.

'Sorry. By the way, what House are we drawn against in the first round?'

'Webster's.'

'Ripping. We can smash Webster's. They've got nobody. It'll be rather a good thing having an easy time in our first game. We shall be able to get some idea about the team's play. I shouldn't think we could possibly get beaten by Webster's.'

There was a knock at the door. Wilson came in with a request that he might fetch a book that he had left in the study.

'Oh, Wilson, just the man I wanted to see,' said the Bishop. 'Wilson, you're playing against Webster's next week.'

'By Jove,' said Wilson, 'am I really?'

He had spent days in working out on little slips of paper during school his exact chances of getting a place in the House team. Recently, however, he had almost ceased to hope. He had reckoned on at least eight of the senior study being chosen before him.

'Yes,' said the Bishop, 'you must buck up. Practise fielding every minute of your spare time. Anybody'll hit you up catches if you ask them.'

'Right,' said Wilson, 'I will.'

'All right, then. Go, and tell Lee that I want to see him.'

74

'Lee,' said the Bishop, when that worthy appeared, 'I wanted to see you, to tell you you're playing for the House against Webster's. Thought you might like to know.'

'By Jove,' said Lee, 'am I really?'

'Yes. Buck up with your fielding.'

'Right,' said Lee.

'That's all. If you're going downstairs, you might tell Adams to come up.'

For a quarter of an hour the Bishop interviewed the junior members of his team, and impressed on each of them the absolute necessity of bucking up with his fielding. And each of them protested that the matter should receive his best consideration.

'Well, they're keen enough anyway,' said Marriott, as the door closed behind Carstairs, the last of the new recruits, 'and that's the great thing. Hullo, who's that? I thought you had worked through the lot. Come in!'

A small form appeared in the doorway, carrying in its right hand a neatly-folded note.

'Monk told me to give you this, Gethryn.'

'Half a second,' said the Bishop, as the youth made for the door.

'There may be an answer.'

'Monk said there wouldn't be one.'

'Oh. No, it's all right. There isn't an answer.'

The door closed. The Bishop laughed, and threw the note over to Reece.

'Recognize it?'

Reece examined the paper.

'It's a fair copy. The one Monk showed me was rather smudged. I suppose they thought you might be hurt if you got an inky round-robin. Considerate chap, Monk.'

'Let's have a look,' said Marriott. 'By Jove. I say, listen to this bit. Like Macaulay, isn't it?'

He read extracts from the ultimatum.

'Let's have it,' said Gethryn, stretching out a hand.

'Not much. I'm going to keep it, and have it framed.'

'All right. I'm going down now to put up the list.'

When he had returned to the study, Monk and Danvers came quietly downstairs to look at the notice-board. It was dark in the passage, and Monk had to strike a light before he could see to read.

'By George,' he said, as the match flared up, 'Reece was right. He has.'

'Well, there's one consolation,' commented Danvers viciously, 'they can't possibly get that cup now. They'll have to put us in again soon, you see if they don't.'

"M, yes,' said Monk doubtfully.

[14]

NORRIS TAKES A SHORT HOLIDAY

'It's all rot,' observed Pringle, 'to say that they haven't a chance, because they have.'

He and Lorimer were passing through the cricket-field on their way back from an early morning visit to the baths, and had stopped to look at Leicester's House team (revised version) taking its daily hour of fielding practice. They watched the performance keenly and critically, as spies in an enemy's camp.

'Who said they hadn't a chance?' said Lorimer. 'I didn't.'

'Oh, everybody. The chaps call them the Kindergarten and the Kids' Happy League, and things of that sort. Rot, I call it. They seem to forget that you only want two or three really good men in a team if the rest can field. Look at our crowd. They've all either got their colours, or else are just outside the teams, and I swear you can't rely on one of them to hold the merest sitter right into his hands.'

On the subject of fielding in general, and catching in particular, Pringle was feeling rather sore. In the match which his House had just won against Browning's, he had put himself on to bowl in the second innings. He was one of those bowlers who manage to capture from six to ten wickets in the course of a season, and the occasions on which he bowled really well were few. On this occasion he had bowled excellently, and it had annoyed him when five catches, five soft, gentle catches, were missed off him in the course of four overs. As he watched the crisp, clean fielding which was shown by the very smallest of Leicester's small 'tail', he felt that he would rather have any of that despised eight on his side than any of the School House lights except Baynes and Lorimer.

'Our lot's all right, really,' said Lorimer, in answer to Pringle's sweeping condemnation. 'Everybody has his off days. They'll be all right next match.'

'Doubt it,' replied Pringle. 'It's all very well for you. You bowl to hit the sticks. I don't. Now just watch these kids for a moment. Now! Look! No, he couldn't have got to that. Wait a second. Now!'

Gethryn had skied one into the deep. Wilson, Burgess, and Carstairs all started for it.

'Burgess,' called the Bishop.

The other two stopped dead. Burgess ran on and made the catch.

'Now, there you are,' said Pringle, pointing his moral, 'see how those two kids stopped when Gethryn called. If that had happened in one of our matches, you'd have had half a dozen men rotting about underneath the ball, and getting in one another's way, and then probably winding up by everybody leaving the catch to everybody else.'

'Oh, come on,' said Lorimer, 'you're getting morbid. Why the dickens didn't you think of having our fellows out for fielding practice, if you're so keen on it?'

'They wouldn't have come. When a chap gets colours, he seems to think he's bought the place. You can't drag a Second Eleven man out of his bed before breakfast to improve his fielding. He thinks it can't be improved. They're a heart-breaking crew.'

'Good,' said Lorimer, 'I suppose that includes me?'

'No. You're a model man. I have seen you hold a catch now and then.'

'Thanks. Oh, I say, I gave in the poem yesterday. I hope the deuce it won't get the prize. I hope they won't spot, either, that I didn't write the thing.'

'Not a chance,' said Pringle complacently, 'you're all right. Don't you worry yourself.'

Webster's, against whom Leicester's had been drawn in the opening round of the House matches, had three men in their team, and only three, who knew how to hold a bat. It was the slackest House in the School, and always had been. It did not cause any overwhelming surprise, accordingly, when Leicester's beat them without fatigue by an innings and a hundred and twenty-one runs. Webster's won the toss, and made thirty-five. For Leicester's, Reece and Gethryn scored fifty and sixty-two respectively, and Marriott fifty-three not out. They then, with two wickets down, declared, and rattled Webster's out for seventy. The public, which had had its eye on the team, in order to see how its tail was likely to shape, was disappointed. The only definite fact that could be gleaned from the match was that the junior members of the team were not to be despised in the field. The early morning field-outs had had their effect. Adams especially shone, while Wilson at cover and Burgess in the deep recalled Jessop and Tyldesley.

The School made a note of the fact. So did the Bishop. He summoned the eight juniors *seriatim* to his study, and administered much praise, coupled with the news that fielding before breakfast would go on as usual.

Leicester's had drawn against Jephson's in the second round. Norris's lot had beaten Cooke's by, curiously enough, almost exactly the same margin as that by which Leicester's had defeated Webster's. It was generally considered that this match would decide Leicester's chances for the cup. If they could beat a really hot team like Jephson's, it was reasonable to suppose that they would do the same to the rest of the Houses, though the School House would have to be reckoned with. But the School House, as Pringle had observed, was weak in the field. It was not a coherent team. Individually its members were good, but they did not play together as Leicester's did.

But the majority of the School did not think seriously of their chances. Except for Pringle, who, as has been mentioned before, always made a point of thinking differently from everyone else, no one really believed that they would win the cup, or even appear in the final. How could a team whose tail began at the fall of the second wicket defeat teams which, like the School House, had no real tail at all?

Norris supported this view. It was for this reason that when, at breakfast on the day on which Jephson's were due to play Leicester's, he received an invitation from one of his many uncles to spend a weekend at his house, he decided to accept it.

This uncle was a man of wealth. After winning two fortunes on the Stock Exchange and losing them both, he had at length amassed a third, with which he retired in triumph to the country, leaving Throgmorton Street to exist as best it could without him. He had bought a 'show-place' at a village which lay twenty miles by rail to the east of Beckford, and it had always been Norris's wish to see this show-place, a house which was said to combine the hoariest of antiquity with a variety of modern comforts.

Merely to pay a flying visit there would be good. But his uncle held out an additional attraction. If Norris could catch the one-forty from Horton, he would arrive just in time to take part in a cricket match, that day being the day of the annual encounter with the neighbouring village of Pudford. The rector of Pudford, the opposition captain, so wrote Norris's uncle, had by underhand means lured down three really decent players from Oxford—not Blues, but almost—who had come to the village ostensibly to read classics with him as their coach, but in reality for the sole purpose of snatching from Little Bindlebury (his own village) the laurels they had so nobly earned the year before. He had heard that Norris was captaining the Beckford team this year, and had an average of thirty-eight point nought three two, so would he come and make thirty-eight point nought three two for Little Bindlebury?

'This,' thought Norris, 'is Fame. This is where I spread myself. I must be in this at any price.'

He showed the letter to Baker.

'What a pity,' said Baker.

'What's a pity?'

'That you won't be able to go. It seems rather a catch.'

'Can't go?' said Norris; 'my dear sir, you're talking through your hat. Think I'm going to refuse an invitation like this? Not if I know it. I'm going to toddle off to Jephson, get an exeat, and catch that one-forty. And if I don't paralyse the Pudford bowling, I'll shoot myself.'

'But the House match! Leicester's! This afternoon!' gurgled the amazed

Baker.

'Oh, hang Leicester's. Surely the rest of you can lick the Kids' Happy League without my help. If you can't, you ought to be ashamed of yourselves. I've chosen you a wicket with my own hands, fit to play a test match on.'

'Of course we ought to lick them. But you can never tell at cricket what's going to happen. We oughtn't to run any risks when we've got such a good chance of winning the pot. Why, it's centuries since we won the pot. Don't you go.'

'I must, man. It's the chance of a lifetime.'

Baker tried another method of attack.

'Besides,' he said, 'you don't suppose Jephson'll let you off to play in a beastly little village game when there's a House match on?'

'He must never know!' hissed Norris, after the manner of the Surrey-side villain.

'He's certain to ask why you want to get off so early.'

'I shall tell him my uncle particularly wishes me to come early.'

'Suppose he asks why?'

'I shall say I can't possibly imagine.'

'Oh, well, if you're going to tell lies—'

'Not at all. Merely a diplomatic evasion. I'm not bound to go and sob out my secrets on Jephson's waistcoat.'

Baker gave up the struggle with a sniff. Norris went to Mr Jephson and got leave to spend the week-end at his uncle's. The interview went without a hitch, as Norris had prophesied.

'You will miss the House match, Norris, then?' said Mr Jephson.

'I'm afraid so, sir. But Mr Leicester's are very weak.'

'H'm. Reece, Marriott, and Gethryn are a good beginning.'

'Yes, sir. But they've got nobody else. Their tail starts after those three.'

'Very well. But it seems a pity.'

'Thank you, sir,' said Norris, wisely refraining from discussing the matter. He had got his exeat, which was what he had come for.

In all the annals of Pudford and Little Bindlebury cricket there had never been such a match as that year's. The rector of Pudford and his three Oxford experts performed prodigies with the bat, prodigies, that is to say, judged from the standpoint of ordinary Pudford scoring, where double figures were the exception rather than the rule.

The rector, an elderly, benevolent-looking gentleman, played with astounding caution and still more remarkable luck for seventeen. Finally, after he had been in an hour and ten minutes, mid-on accepted the eighth easy chance offered to him, and the ecclesiastic had to retire. The three 'Varsity men knocked up a hundred between them, and the complete total was no less than a hundred and thirty-four.

Then came the sensation of the day. After three wickets had fallen for ten runs, Norris and the Little Bindlebury curate, an old Cantab, stayed together and knocked off the deficit.

Norris's contribution of seventy-eight not out was for many a day the sole topic of conversation over the evening pewter at the 'Little Bindlebury Arms'. A non-enthusiast, who tried on one occasion to introduce the topic of Farmer Giles's grey pig, found himself the most unpopular man in the village.

On the Monday morning Norris returned to Jephson's, with pride in his heart and a sovereign in his pocket, the latter the gift of his excellent uncle.

He had had, he freely admitted to himself, a good time. His uncle had done him well, exceedingly well, and he looked forward to going to the show-place again in the near future. In the meantime he felt a languid desire to know how the House match was going on. They must almost have finished the first innings, he thought—unless Jephson's had run up a very big score, and kept their opponents in the field all the afternoon.

'Hullo, Baker,' he said, tramping breezily into the study, 'I've had the time of a lifetime. Great, simply! No other word for it. How's the match getting on?'

Baker looked up from the book he was reading.

'What match?' he enquired coldly.

'House match, of course, you lunatic. What match did you think I meant?

How's it going on?'

'It's not going on,' said Baker, 'it's stopped.'

'You needn't be a funny goat,' said Norris complainingly. 'You know what I mean. What happened on Saturday?'

'They won the toss,' began Baker slowly.

'Yes?'

'And went in and made a hundred and twenty.'

'Good. I told you they were no use. A hundred and twenty's rotten.'

'Then we went in, and made twenty-one.'

'Hundred and twenty-one.'

'No. Just a simple twenty-one without any trimmings of any sort.'

'But, man! How? Why? How on earth did it happen?'

'Gethryn took eight for nine. Does that seem to make it any clearer?'

'Eight for nine? Rot.'

'Show you the score-sheet if you care to see it. In the second innings—'

'Oh, you began a second innings?'

'Yes. We also finished it. We scored rather freely in the second innings. Ten was on the board before the fifth wicket fell. In the end we fairly collared the bowling, and ran up a total of forty-eight.'

Norris took a seat, and tried to grapple with the situation.

'Forty-eight! Look here, Baker, swear you're not ragging.'

Baker took a green scoring-book from the shelf and passed it to him.

'Look for yourself,' he said.

Norris looked. He looked long and earnestly. Then he handed the book back.

'Then they've won!' he said blankly.

'How do you guess these things?' observed Baker with some bitterness.

'Well, you are a crew,' said Norris. 'Getting out for twenty-one and forty-eight! I see Gethryn got nine for thirty in the second innings. He seems to have been on the spot. I suppose the wicket suited him.'

'If you can call it a wicket. Next time you specially select a pitch for the House to play on, I wish you'd hunt up something with some slight pretensions to decency.'

'Why, what was wrong with the pitch? It was a bit worn, that was all.'

'If,' said Baker, 'you call having holes three inches deep just where every ball pitches being a bit worn, I suppose it was. Anyhow, it would have been almost as well, don't you think, if you'd stopped and played for the House, instead of going off to your rotten village match? You were sick enough when Gethryn went off in the M.C.C. match.'

'Oh, curse,' said Norris.

For he had been hoping against hope that the parallel nature of the two incidents would be less apparent to other people than it was to himself.

And so it came about that Leicester's passed successfully through the first two rounds and soared into the dizzy heights of the semi-final.

[15]

VERSUS CHARCHESTER (AT CHARCHESTER)

From the fact that he had left his team so basely in the lurch on the day of an important match, a casual observer might have imagined that Norris did not really care very much whether his House won the cup or not. But this was not the case. In reality the success of Jephson's was a very important matter to him. A sudden whim had induced him to accept his uncle's invitation, but now that that acceptance had had such disastrous results, he felt inclined to hire a sturdy menial by the hour to kick him till he felt better. To a person in such a frame of mind there are three methods of consolation. He can commit suicide, he can take to drink, or he can occupy his mind with other matters, and cure himself by fixing his attention steadily on some object, and devoting his whole energies to the acquisition of the same.

Norris chose the last method. On the Saturday week following his performance for Little Bindlebury, the Beckford Eleven was due to journey to Charchester, to play the return match against that school on their opponents' ground, and Norris resolved that that match should be won. For the next week the team practised assiduously, those members of it who were not playing in House matches spending every afternoon at the nets. The treatment was not without its effect. The team had been a good one before. Now every one of the eleven seemed to be at the very summit of his powers. New and hitherto unsuspected strokes began to be developed, leg glances which recalled the Hove and Ranjitsinhji, late cuts of Palairetical brilliance. In short, all Nature may be said to have smiled, and by the end of the week Norris was beginning to be almost cheerful once more. And then, on the Monday before the match, Samuel Wilberforce Gosling came to school with his right arm in a sling. Norris met him at the School gates, rubbed his eyes to see whether it was not after all some horrid optical illusion, and finally, when the stern truth came home to him, almost swooned with anguish.

'What? How? Why?' he enquired lucidly.

The injured Samuel smiled feebly.

'I'm fearfully sorry, Norris,' he said.

'Don't say you can't play on Saturday,' moaned Norris.

'Frightfully sorry. I know it's a bit of a sickener. But I don't see how I can, really. The doctor says I shan't be able to play for a couple of weeks.'

Now that the blow had definitely fallen, Norris was sufficiently himself again to be able to enquire into the matter.

'How on earth did you do it? How did it happen?'

Gosling looked guiltier than ever.

'It was on Saturday evening,' he said. 'We were ragging about at home a bit, you know, and my young sister wanted me to send her down a few balls. Somebody had given her a composition bean and a bat, and she's been awfully keen on the game ever since she got them.'

'I think it's simply sickening the way girls want to do everything we do,' said Norris disgustedly.

Gosling spoke for the defence.

'Well, she's only thirteen. You can't blame the kid. Seemed to me a jolly healthy symptom. Laudable ambition and that sort of thing.'

'Well?'

'Well, I sent down one or two. She played 'em like a book. Bit inclined to pull. All girls are. So I put in a long hop on the off, and she let go at it like Jessop. She's got a rattling stroke in mid-on's direction. Well, the bean came whizzing back rather wide on the right. I doubled across to bring off a beefy c-and-b, and the bally thing took me right on the tips of the fingers. Those composition balls hurt like blazes, I can tell you. Smashed my second finger simply into hash, and I couldn't grip a ball now to save my life. Much less bowl. I'm awfully sorry. It's a shocking nuisance.'

Norris agreed with him. It was more than a nuisance. It was a staggerer. Now that Gethryn no longer figured for the First Eleven, Gosling was the School's one hope. Baynes was good on his wicket, but the wickets he liked were the sea-of-mud variety, and this summer fine weather had set in early and continued. Lorimer was also useful, but not to be mentioned in the same breath as the great Samuel. The former was good, the latter would be good in a year or so. His proper sphere of action was the tail. If the first pair of bowlers could dismiss five good batsmen, Lorimer's fast, straight deliveries usually accounted for the rest. But there had to be somebody to pave the way for him. He was essentially a change bowler. It is hardly to be wondered at that Norris very soon began to think wistfully of the Bishop, who was just now doing such great things with the ball, wasting his sweetness on the desert air of the House matches. Would it be consistent with his dignity to invite him back into the team? It was a nice point. With some persons there might be a risk. But Gethryn, as he knew perfectly well, was not the sort of fellow to rub in the undeniable fact that the School team could not get along without him. He had half decided to ask him to play against Charchester, when Gosling suggested the very same thing.

'Why don't you have Gethryn in again?' he said. 'You've stood him out against the O.B.s and the Masters. Surely that's enough. Especially as he's miles the best bowler in the School.'

'Bar yourself.'

'Not a bit. He can give me points. You take my tip and put him in again.'

'Think he'd play if I put him down? Because, you know, I'm dashed if

I'm going to do any grovelling and that sort of thing.'

'Certain to, I should think. Anyhow, it's worth trying.'

Pringle, on being consulted, gave the same opinion, and Norris was convinced. The list went up that afternoon, and for the first time since the M.C.C. match Gethryn's name appeared in its usual place.

'Norris is learning wisdom in his old age,' said Marriott to the Bishop, as they walked over to the House that evening.

Leicester's were in the middle of their semi-final, and looked like winning it.

'I was just wondering what to do about it,' said Gethryn. 'What would you do? Play, do you think?'

'Play! My dear man, what else did you propose to do? You weren't thinking of refusing?'

'I was.'

'But, man! That's rank treason. If you're put down to play for the School you must play. There's no question about it. If Norris knocked you down with one hand and put you up on the board with the other, you'd have to play all the same. You mustn't have any feelings where the School is concerned. Nobody's ever refused to play in a first match. It's one of the things you can't do. Norris hasn't given you much of a time lately, I admit. Still, you must lump that. Excuse sermon. I hope it's done you good.'

'Very well. I'll play. It's rather rot, though.'

'No, it's all right, really. It's only that you've got into a groove. You're so used to doing the heavy martyr, that the sudden change has knocked you out rather. Come and have an ice before the shop shuts.'

So Gethryn came once more into the team, and travelled down to Charchester with the others. And at this point a painful alternative faces me. I have to choose between truth and inclination. I should like to say that the Bishop eclipsed himself, and broke all previous records in the Charchester match. By the rules of the dramatic, nothing else is possible. But truth, though it crush me, and truth compels me to admit that his performance was in reality distinctly mediocre. One of his weak points as a bowler was that he was at sea when opposed to a left-hander. Many bowlers have this failing. Some strange power seems to compel them to bowl solely on the leg side, and nothing but long hops and full pitches. It was so in the case of Gethryn. Charchester won the toss, and batted first on a perfect wicket. The first pair of batsmen were the captain, a great bat, who had scored seventy-three not out against Beckford in the previous match, and a left-handed fiend. Baynes's leg-breaks were useless on a wicket which, from the hardness of it, might have been constructed of asphalt, and the rubbish the Bishop rolled up to the left-handed artiste was painful to witness. At four o'clock—the match had started at half-past eleven—the Charchester captain reached his century, and was almost immediately stumped off Baynes. The Bishop bowled the next man first ball, the one bright spot in his afternoon's performance. Then came another long stand, against which the Beckford bowling raged in vain. At five o'clock, Charchester by that time having made two hundred and forty-one for two wickets, the left-hander ran into three figures, and the captain promptly declared the innings closed. Beckford's only chance was to play for a draw, and in this they succeeded. When stumps were drawn at a quarter to seven, the score was a hundred and three, and five wickets were down. The Bishop had the satisfaction of being not out with twenty-eight to his credit, but nothing less than a century would have been sufficient to soothe him after his shocking bowling performance. Pringle, who during the luncheon interval had encountered his young friends the Ashbys, and had been duly taunted by them on the subject of leather-hunting, was top scorer with forty-one. Norris, I regret to say, only made three, running himself out in his second over. As the misfortune could not, by any stretch of imagination, be laid at anybody else's door but his own, he was decidedly savage. The team returned to Beckford rather footsore, very disgusted, and abnormally silent. Norris sulked by himself at one end of the saloon carriage, and the Bishop sulked by himself at the other end, and even Marriott forbore to treat the situation lightly. It was a mournful home-coming. No cheering wildly as the brake drove to the College from Horton, no shouting of the School song in various keys as they passed through the big gates. Simply silence. And except when putting him on to bowl, or taking him off, or moving him in the field, Norris had not spoken a word to the Bishop the whole afternoon.

It was shortly after this disaster that Mr Mortimer Wells came to stay with the Headmaster. Mr Mortimer Wells was a brilliant and superior young man, who was at some pains to be a cynic. He was an old pupil of the Head's in the days before he had succeeded to the rule of Beckford. He had the reputation of being a 'ripe' scholar, and to him had been deputed the task of judging the poetical outbursts of the bards of the Upper Fifth, with the object of awarding to the most deserving—or, perhaps, to the least undeserving—the handsome prize bequeathed by his open-handed highness, the Rajah of Seltzerpore.

This gentleman sat with his legs stretched beneath the Headmaster's generous table. Dinner had come to an end, and a cup of coffee, acting in co-operation with several glasses of port and an excellent cigar, had inspired him to hold forth on the subject of poetry prizes. He held forth.

'The poetry prize system,' said he—it is astonishing what nonsense a man, ordinarily intelligent, will talk after dinner—'is on exactly the same principle as those penny-in-the-slot machines that you see at stations. You insert your penny. You set your prize subject. In the former case you hope for wax vestas, and you get butterscotch. In the latter, you hope for something at least readable, and you get the most complete, terrible, uninspired twaddle that was ever written on paper. The boy mind'—here the ash of his cigar fell off on to his waistcoat—'the merely boy mind is incapable of poetry.'

From which speech the shrewd reader will infer that Mr Mortimer Wells was something of a prig. And perhaps, altogether shrewd reader, you're right.

Mr Lawrie, the master of the Sixth, who had been asked to dinner to meet the great man, disagreed as a matter of principle. He was one of those men who will take up a cause from pure love of argument.

'I think you're wrong, sir. I'm perfectly convinced you're wrong.'

Mr Wells smiled in his superior way, as if to say that it was a pity that Mr Lawrie was so foolish, but that perhaps he could not help it.

'Ah,' he said, 'but you have not had to wade through over thirty of these gems in a single week. I have. I can assure you your views would undergo a change if you could go through what I have. Let me read you a selection. If that does not convert you, nothing will. If you will excuse me for a moment, Beckett, I will leave the groaning board, and fetch the manuscripts.'

He left the room, and returned with a pile of paper, which he deposited in front of him on the table.

'Now,' he said, selecting the topmost manuscript, 'I will take no unfair advantage. I will read you the very pick of the bunch. None of the other—er—poems come within a long way of this. It is a case of Eclipse first and the rest nowhere. The author, the gifted author, is a boy of the name of Lorimer, whom I congratulate on taking the Rajah's prize. I drain this cup of coffee to him. Are you ready? Now, then.'

He cleared his throat.

A DISPUTED AUTHORSHIP

'One moment,' said Mr Lawrie, 'might I ask what is the subject of the poem?'

'Death of Dido,' said the Headmaster. 'Good, hackneyed, evergreen subject, mellow with years. Go on, Wells.'

Mr Wells began.

> Queen of Tyre, ancient Tyre,
> Whilom mistress of the wave.

Mr Lawrie, who had sunk back into the recesses of his chair in an attitude of attentive repose, sat up suddenly with a start.

'What!' he cried.

'Hullo,' said Mr Wells, 'has the beauty of the work come home to you already?'

'You notice,' he said, as he repeated the couplet, 'that flaws begin to appear in the gem right from the start. It was rash of Master Lorimer to attempt such a difficult metre. Plucky, but rash. He should have stuck to blank verse. Tyre, you notice, two syllables to rhyme with "deny her" in line three. "What did fortune e'er deny her? Were not all her warriors brave?" That last line seems to me distinctly weak. I don't know how it strikes you.'

'You're hypercritical, Wells,' said the Head. 'Now, for a boy I consider that a very good beginning. What do you say, Lawrie?'

'I—er. Oh, I think I am hardly a judge.'

'To resume,' said Mr Mortimer Wells. He resumed, and ran through the remaining verses of the poem with comments. When he had finished, he remarked that, in his opinion a whiff of fresh air would not hurt him. If the Headmaster would excuse him, he would select another of those excellent cigars, and smoke it out of doors.

'By all means,' said the Head; 'I think I won't join you myself, but perhaps Lawrie will.'

'No, thank you. I think I will remain. Yes, I think I will remain.'

Mr Wells walked jauntily out of the room. When the door had shut, Mr

Lawrie coughed nervously.

'Another cigar, Lawrie?'

'I—er—no, thank you. I want to ask you a question. What is your candid opinion of those verses Mr Wells was reading just now?'

The Headmaster laughed.

'I don't think Wells treated them quite fairly. In my opinion they were distinctly promising. For a boy in the Upper Fifth, you understand. Yes, on the whole they showed distinct promise.'

'They were mine,' said Mr Lawrie.

'Yours! I don't understand. How were they yours?'

'I wrote them. Every word of them.'

'You wrote them! But, my dear Lawrie—'

'I don't wonder that you are surprised. For my own part I am amazed, simply amazed. How the boy—I don't even remember his name—contrived to get hold of them, I have not the slightest conception. But that he did so contrive is certain. The poem is word for word, literally word for word, the same as one which I wrote when I was at Cambridge.'

'You don't say so!'

'Yes. It can hardly be a coincidence.'

'Hardly,' said the Head. 'Are you certain of this?'

'Perfectly certain. I am not eager to claim the authorship, I can assure you, especially after Mr Wells's very outspoken criticisms, but there is nothing else to be done. The poem appeared more than a dozen years ago, in a small book called *The Dark Horse*.'

'Ah! Something in the Whyte Melville style, I suppose?'

'No,' said Mr Lawrie sharply. 'No. Certainly not. They were serious poems, tragical most of them. I had them collected, and published them at my own expense. Very much at my own expense. I used a pseudonym, I am thankful to say. As far as I could ascertain, the total sale amounted to eight copies. I have never felt the very slightest inclination to repeat the performance. But how this boy managed to see the book is more than I can explain. He can hardly have bought it. The price was half-a-guinea. And there is certainly no copy in the School library. The thing is a mystery.'

'A mystery that must be solved,' said the Headmaster. 'The fact remains that he did see the book, and it is very serious. Wholesale plagiarism of this description should be kept for the School magazine. It should not be allowed to spread to poetry prizes. I must see Lorimer about this tomorrow. Perhaps he can throw some light upon the matter.'

When, in the course of morning school next day, the School porter entered the Upper Fifth form-room and informed Mr Sims, who was engaged in trying to drive the beauties of Plautus' colloquial style into the Upper Fifth brain, that the Headmaster wished to see Lorimer, Lorimer's conscience was so abnormally good that for the life of him he could not think why he had been sent for. As far as he could remember, there was no possible way in which the authorities could get at him. If he had been in the habit of smoking out of bounds in lonely fields and deserted barns, he might have felt uneasy. But whatever his failings, that was not one of them. It could not be anything about bounds, because he had been so busy with cricket that he had had no time to break them this term. He walked into the presence, glowing with conscious rectitude. And no sooner was he inside than the Headmaster, with three simple words, took every particle of starch out of his anatomy.

'Sit down, Lorimer,' he said.

There are many ways of inviting a person to seat himself. The genial 'take a pew' of one's equal inspires confidence. The raucous 'sit down in front' of the frenzied pit, when you stand up to get a better view of the stage, is not so pleasant. But worst of all is the icy 'sit down' of the annoyed headmaster. In his mouth the words take to themselves new and sinister meanings. They seem to accuse you of nameless crimes, and to warn you that anything you may say will be used against you as evidence.

'Why have I sent for you, Lorimer?'

A nasty question that, and a very favourite one of the Rev. Mr Beckett, Headmaster of Beckford. In nine cases out of ten, the person addressed, paralysed with nervousness, would give himself away upon the instant, and confess everything. Lorimer, however, was saved by the fact that he had nothing to confess. He stifled an inclination to reply 'because the woodpecker would peck her', or words to that effect, and maintained a pallid silence.

'Have you ever heard of a book called *The Dark Horse*, Lorimer?'

Lorimer began to feel that the conversation was too deep for him. After opening in the conventional 'judge-then-placed-the-black-cap-on-his-head' manner, his assailant had suddenly begun to babble lightly of sporting literature. He began to entertain doubts of the Headmaster's sanity. It would not have added greatly to his mystification if the Head had gone on to insist that he was the Emperor of Peru, and worked solely by electricity.

The Headmaster, for his part, was also surprised. He had worked for dismay, conscious guilt, confessions, and the like, instead of blank amazement. He, too, began to have his doubts. Had Mr Lawrie been mistaken? It was not likely, but it was barely possible. In which case the interview had better be brought to an abrupt stop until he had made inquiries. The situation was at a deadlock.

90

Fortunately at this point half-past twelve struck, and the bell rang for the end of morning school. The situation was saved, and the tension relaxed.

'You may go, Lorimer,' said the Head, 'I will send for you later.'

He swept out of the room, and Lorimer raced over to the House to inform Pringle that the Headmaster had run suddenly mad, and should by rights be equipped with a strait-waistcoat.

'You never saw such a man,' he said, 'hauled me out of school in the middle of a Plautus lesson, dumps me down in a chair, and then asks me if I've read some weird sporting novel or other.'

'Sporting novel! My dear man!'

'Well, it sounded like it from the title.'

'The title. Oh!'

'What's up?'

Pringle had leaped to his feet as if he had suddenly discovered that he was sitting on something red-hot. His normal air of superior calm had vanished. He was breathless with excitement. A sudden idea had struck him with the force of a bullet.

'What was the title he asked you if you'd read the book of?' he demanded incoherently.

'*The Derby Winner.*'

Pringle sat down again, relieved.

'Oh. Are you certain?'

'No, of course it wasn't that. I was only ragging. The real title was *The Dark Horse*. Hullo, what's up now? Have you got 'em too?'

'What's up? I'll tell you. We're done for. Absolutely pipped. That's what's the matter.'

'Hang it, man, do give us a chance. Why can't you explain, instead of sitting there talking like that? Why are we done? What have we done, anyway?'

'The poem, of course, the prize poem. I forgot, I never told you. I hadn't time to write anything of my own, so I cribbed it straight out of a book called *The Dark Horse*. Now do you see?'

Lorimer saw. He grasped the whole unpainted beauty of the situation in a flash, and for some moments it rendered him totally unfit for intellectual conversation. When he did speak his observation was brief, but it teemed with condensed meaning. It was the conversational parallel to the ox in the tea-cup.

'My aunt!' he said.

'There'll be a row about this,' said Pringle.

91

'What am I to say when he has me in this afternoon? He said he would.'

'Let the whole thing out. No good trying to hush it up. He may let us down easy if you're honest about it.'

It relieved Lorimer to hear Pringle talk about 'us'. It meant that he was not to be left to bear the assault alone. Which, considering that the whole trouble was, strictly speaking, Pringle's fault, was only just.

'But how am I to explain? I can't reel off a long yarn all about how you did it all, and so on. It would be too low.'

'I know,' said Pringle, 'I've got it. Look here, on your way to the Old

Man's room you pass the Remove door. Well, when you pass, drop some

money. I'll be certain to hear it, as I sit next the door. And then I'll ask to leave the room, and we'll go up together.'

'Good man, Pringle, you're a genius. Thanks, awfully.'

But as it happened, this crafty scheme was not found necessary. The blow did not fall till after lock-up.

Lorimer being in the Headmaster's House, it was possible to interview him without the fuss and advertisement inseparable from a 'sending for during school'. Just as he was beginning his night-work, the butler came with a message that he was wanted in the Headmaster's part of the House.

'It was only Mr Lorimer as the master wished to see,' said the butler, as Pringle rose to accompany his companion in crime.

'That's all right,' said Pringle, 'the Headmaster's always glad to see me. I've got a standing invitation. He'll understand.'

At first, when he saw two where he had only sent for one, the Headmaster did not understand at all, and said so. He had prepared to annihilate Lorimer hip and thigh, for he was now convinced that his blank astonishment at the mention of *The Dark Horse* during their previous interview had been, in the words of the bard, a mere veneer, a wile of guile. Since the morning he had seen Mr Lawrie again, and had with his own eyes compared the two poems, the printed and the written, the author by special request having hunted up a copy of that valuable work, *The Dark Horse*, from the depths of a cupboard in his rooms.

His astonishment melted before Pringle's explanation, which was brief and clear, and gave way to righteous wrath. In well-chosen terms he harangued the two criminals. Finally he perorated.

'There is only one point which tells in your favour. You have not attempted concealment.' (Pringle nudged Lorimer surreptitiously at this.) 'And I may add that I believe that, as you say, you did not desire actually to win the prize by underhand means. But I cannot overlook such an offence. It is serious. Most serious. You will, both of you, go into extra lesson for the remaining Saturdays of the term.'

Extra lesson meant that instead of taking a half-holiday on Saturday like an ordinary law-abiding individual, you treated the day as if it were a full-school day, and worked from two till four under the eye of the Headmaster. Taking into consideration everything, the punishment was not an extraordinarily severe one, for there were only two more Saturdays to the end of term, and the sentence made no mention of the Wednesday half-holidays.

But in effect it was serious indeed. It meant that neither Pringle nor Lorimer would be able to play in the final House match against Leicester's, which was fixed to begin on the next Saturday at two o'clock. Among the rules governing the House matches was one to the effect that no House might start a match with less than eleven men, nor might the Eleven be changed during the progress of the match—a rule framed by the Headmaster, not wholly without an eye to emergencies like the present.

'Thank goodness,' said Pringle, 'that there aren't any more First matches. It's bad enough, though, by Jove, as it is. I suppose it's occurred to you that this cuts us out of playing in the final?'

Lorimer said the point had not escaped his notice.

'I wish,' he observed, with simple pathos, 'that I'd got the Rajah of Seltzerpore here now. I'd strangle him. I wonder if the Old Man realizes that he's done his own House out of the cup?'

'Wouldn't care if he did. Still, it's a sickening nuisance. Leicester's are a cert now.'

'Absolute cert,' said Lorimer; 'Baynes can't do all the bowling, especially on a hard wicket, and there's nobody else. As for our batting and fielding—'

'Don't,' said-Pringle gloomily, 'it's too awful.'

On the following Saturday, Leicester's ran up a total in their first innings which put the issue out of doubt, and finished off the game on the Monday by beating the School House by six wickets.

[17]

THE WINTER TERM

It was the first day of the winter term.

The Bishop, as he came back by express, could not help feeling that, after all, life considered as an institution had its points. Things had mended steadily during the last weeks of the term. He had kept up his end as head of the House perfectly. The internal affairs of Leicester's were going as smoothly as oil. And there was the cricket cup to live up to. Nothing pulls a House together more than beating all comers in the field, especially against odds, as Leicester's had done. And then Monk and Danvers had left. That had set the finishing touch to a good term's work. The Mob were no longer a power in the land. Waterford remained, but a subdued, benevolent Waterford, with a wonderful respect for law and order. Yes, as far as the House was concerned, Gethryn felt no apprehensions. As regarded the School at large, things were bound to come right in time. A school has very little memory. And in the present case the Bishop, being second man in the Fifteen, had unusual opportunities of righting himself in the eyes of the multitude. In the winter term cricket is forgotten. Football is the only game that counts.

And to round off the whole thing, when he entered his study he found a letter on the table. It was from Farnie, and revealed two curious and interesting facts. Firstly he had left, and Beckford was to know him no more. Secondly—this was even more remarkable—he possessed a conscience.

'Dear Gethryn,' ran the letter, 'I am writing to tell you my father is sending me to a school in France, so I shall not come back to Beckford. I am sorry about the M.C.C. match, and I enclose the four pounds you lent me. I utterly bar the idea of going to France. It's beastly, yours truly, R. Farnie.'

The money mentioned was in the shape of a cheque, signed by Farnie senior.

Gethryn was distinctly surprised. That all this time remorse like a worm i' the bud should have been feeding upon his uncle's damask cheek, as it were, he had never suspected. His relative's demeanour since the M.C.C. match had, it is true, been considerably toned down, but this he had attributed to natural causes, not unnatural ones like conscience. As for the four pounds, he had set it down as a bad debt. To get it back was like coming suddenly into an unexpected fortune. He began to think that there must have been some good in Farnie after all, though he was fain to admit that without the aid of a microscope the human eye might well have been excused for failing to detect it.

His next thought was that there was nothing now to prevent him telling the whole story to Reece and Marriott. Reece, if anybody, deserved to have his curiosity satisfied. The way in which he had abstained from questions at the time of the episode had been nothing short of magnificent. Reece must certainly be told.

Neither Reece nor Marriott had arrived at the moment. Both were in the habit of returning at the latest possible hour, except at the beginning of the summer term. The Bishop determined to reserve his story until the following evening.

Accordingly, when the study kettle was hissing on the Etna, and Wilson was crouching in front of the fire, making toast in his own inimitable style, he embarked upon his narrative.

'I say, Marriott.'

'Hullo.'

'Do you notice a subtle change in me this term? Does my expressive purple eye gleam more brightly than of yore? It does. Exactly so. I feel awfully bucked up. You know that kid Farnie has left?'

'I thought I missed his merry prattle. What's happened to him?'

'Gone to a school in France somewhere.'

'Jolly for France.'

'Awfully. But the point is that now he's gone I can tell you about that M.C.C. match affair. I know you want to hear what really did happen that afternoon.'

Marriott pointed significantly at Wilson, whose back was turned.

'Oh, that's all right,' said Gethryn. 'Wilson.'

'Yes?'

'You mustn't listen. Try and think you're a piece of furniture. See? And if you do happen to overhear anything, you needn't go gassing about it. Follow?'

'All right,' said Wilson, and Gethryn told his tale.

'Jove,' he said, as he finished, 'that's a relief. It's something to have got that off my chest. I do bar keeping a secret.'

'But, I say,' said Marriott.

'Well?'

'Well, it was beastly good of you to do it, and that sort of thing, I suppose. I see that all right. But, my dear man, what a rotten thing to do. A kid like that. A little beast who simply cried out for sacking.'

'Well, at any rate, it's over now. You needn't jump on me. I acted from the best motives. That's what my grandfather, Farnie's *pater*, you know, always used to say when he got at me for anything in the happy days of my childhood. Don't sit there looking like a beastly churchwarden, you ass. Buck up, and take an intelligent interest in things.'

'No, but really, Bishop,' said Marriott, 'you must treat this seriously. You'll have to let the other chaps know about it.'

'How? Put it up on the notice-board? This is to certify that Mr Allan Gethryn, of Leicester's House, Beckford, is dismissed without a stain on his character. You ass, how can I let them know? I seem to see myself doing the boy-hero style of things. My friends, you wronged me, you wronged me very grievously. But I forgive you. I put up with your cruel scorn. I endured it. I steeled myself against it. And now I forgive you profusely, every one of you. Let us embrace. It wouldn't do. You must see that much. Don't be a goat. Is that toast done yet, Wilson?'

Wilson exhibited several pounds of the article in question.

'Good,' said the Bishop. 'You're a great man, Wilson. You can make a small selection of those biscuits, and if you bag all the sugar ones I'll slay you, and then you can go quietly downstairs, and rejoin your sorrowing friends. And don't you go telling them what I've been saying.'

'Rather not,' said Wilson.

He made his small selection, and retired. The Bishop turned to Marriott again.

'I shall tell Reece, because he deserves it, and I rather think I shall tell Gosling and Pringle. Nobody else, though. What's the good of it? Everybody'll forget the whole thing by next season.'

'How about Norris?' asked Marriott.

'Now there you have touched the spot. I can't possibly tell Norris myself. My natural pride is too enormous. Descended from a primordial atomic globule, you know, like Pooh Bah. And I shook hands with a duke once. The man Norris and I, I regret to say, had something of a row on the subject last term. We parted with mutual expressions of hate, and haven't spoken since. What I should like would be for somebody else to tell him all about it. Not you. It would look too much like a put-up job. So don't you go saying anything. Swear.'

'Why not?'

'Because you mustn't. Swear. Let me hear you swear by the bones of your ancestors.'

'All right. I call it awful rot, though.'

'Can't be helped. Painful but necessary. Now I'm going to tell Reece, though I don't expect he'll remember anything about it. Reece never remembers anything beyond his last meal.'

'Idiot,' said Marriott after him as the door closed. 'I don't know, though,' he added to himself.

And, pouring himself out another cup of tea, he pondered deeply over the matter.

Reece heard the news without emotion.

'You're a good sort, Bishop,' he said, 'I knew something of the kind must have happened. It reminds me of a thing that happened to—'

'Yes, it is rather like it, isn't it?' said the Bishop. 'By the way, talking about stories, a chap I met in the holidays told me a ripper. You see, this chap and his brother—'

He discoursed fluently for some twenty minutes. Reece sighed softly, but made no attempt to resume his broken narrative. He was used to this sort of thing.

It was a fortnight later, and Marriott and the Bishop were once more seated in their study waiting for Wilson to get tea ready. Wilson made toast in the foreground. Marriott was in football clothes, rubbing his shin gently where somebody had kicked it in the scratch game that afternoon. After rubbing for a few moments in silence, he spoke suddenly.

'You must tell Norris,' he said. 'It's all rot.'

'I can't.'

'Then I shall.'

'No, don't. You swore you wouldn't.'

'Well, but look here. I just want to ask you one question. What sort of a time did you have in that scratch game tonight?'

'Beastly. I touched the ball exactly four times. If I wasn't so awfully ornamental, I don't see what would be the use of my turning out at all. I'm no practical good to the team.'

'Exactly. That's just what I wanted to get at. I don't mean your remark about your being ornamental, but about your never touching the ball. Until you explain matters to Norris, you never will get a decent pass. Norris and you are a rattling good pair of centre threes, but if he never gives you a pass, I don't see how we can expect to have any combination in the First. It's no good my slinging out the ball if the centres stick to it like glue directly they get it, and refuse to give it up. It's simply sickening.'

Marriott played half for the First Fifteen, and his soul was in the business.

'But, my dear chap,' said Gethryn, 'you don't mean to tell me that a man like Norris would purposely rot up the First's combination because he happened to have had a row with the other centre. He's much too decent a fellow.'

'No. I don't mean that exactly. What he does is this. I've watched him. He gets the ball. He runs with it till his man is on him, and then he thinks of passing. You're backing him up. He sees you, and says to himself, "I can't pass to that cad"—'

'Meaning me?'

'Meaning you.'

'Thanks awfully.'

'Don't mention it. I'm merely quoting his thoughts, as deduced by me. He says, "I can't pass to that—well, individual, if you prefer it. Where's somebody else?" So he hesitates, and gets tackled, or else slings the ball wildly out to somebody who can't possibly get to it. It's simply infernal. And we play the Nomads tomorrow, too. Something must be done.'

'Somebody ought to tell him. Why doesn't our genial skipper assert his authority?'

'Hill's a forward, you see, and doesn't get an opportunity of noticing it. I can't tell him, of course. I've not got my colours—'

'You're a cert. for them.'

'Hope so. Anyway, I've not got them yet, and Norris has, so I can't very well go slanging him to Hill. Sort of thing rude people would call side.'

'Well, I'll look out tomorrow, and if it's as bad as you think, I'll speak to Hill. It's a beastly thing to have to do.'

'Beastly,' agreed Marriott. 'It's got to be done, though. We can't go through the season without any combination in the three-quarter line, just to spare Norris's feelings.'

'It's a pity, though,' said the Bishop, 'because Norris is a ripping good sort of chap, really. I wish we hadn't had that bust-up last term.'

[18]

THE BISHOP SCORES

At this point Wilson finished the toast, and went out. As he went he thought over what he had just heard. Marriott and

Gethryn frequently talked the most important School politics before him, for they had discovered at an early date that he was a youth of discretion, who could be trusted not to reveal state secrets. But matters now seemed to demand such a revelation. It was a serious thing to do, but there was nobody else to do it, and it obviously must be done, so, by a simple process of reasoning, he ought to do it. Half an hour had to elapse before the bell rang for lock-up. There was plenty of time to do the whole thing and get back to the House before the door was closed. He took his cap, and trotted off to Jephson's.

Norris was alone in his study when Wilson knocked at the door. He seemed surprised to see his visitor. He knew Wilson well by sight, he being captain of the First Eleven and Wilson a distinctly promising junior bat, but this was the first time he had ever exchanged a word of conversation with him.

'Hullo,' he said, putting down his book.

'Oh, I say, Norris,' began Wilson nervously, 'can I speak to you for a minute?'

'All right. Go ahead.'

After two false starts, Wilson at last managed to get the thread of his story. He did not mention Marriott's remarks on football subjects, but confined himself to the story of Farnie and the bicycle ride, as he had heard it from Gethryn on the second evening of the term.

'So that's how it was, you see,' he concluded.

There was a long silence. Wilson sat nervously on the edge of his chair, and Norris stared thoughtfully into the fire.

'So shall I tell him it's all right?' asked Wilson at last.

'Tell who what's all right?' asked Norris politely.

'Oh, er, Gethryn, you know,' replied Wilson, slightly disconcerted. He had had a sort of idea that Norris would have rushed out of the room, sprinted over to Leicester's, and flung himself on the Bishop's bosom in an agony of remorse. He appeared to be taking things altogether too coolly.

'No,' said Norris, 'don't tell him anything. I shall have lots of chances of speaking to him myself if I want to. It isn't as if we were never going to meet again. You'd better cut now. There's the bell just going. Good night.'

'Good night, Norris.'

'Oh, and, I say,' said Norris, as Wilson opened the door, 'I meant to tell you some time ago. If you buck up next cricket season, it's quite possible that you'll get colours of some sort. You might bear that in mind.'

'I will,' said Wilson fervently. 'Good night, Norris. Thanks awfully.'

The Nomads brought down a reasonably hot team against Beckford as a general rule, for the School had a reputation in the football world. They were a big lot this year. Their forwards looked capable, and when, after the School full-back had returned the ball into touch on the half-way line, the line-out had resulted in a hand-ball and a scrum, they proved that appearances were not deceptive. They broke through in a solid mass—the Beckford forwards never somehow seemed to get together properly in the first scrum of a big match—and rushed the ball down the field. Norris fell on it. Another hastily-formed scrum, and the Nomads' front rank was off again. Ten yards nearer the School line there was another halt. Grainger, the Beckford full-back, whose speciality was the stopping of rushes, had curled himself neatly round the ball. Then the School forwards awoke to a sense of their responsibilities. It was time they did, for Beckford was now penned up well within its own twenty-five line, and the Nomad halves were appealing pathetically to their forwards to let that ball out, for goodness' *sake*. But the forwards fancied a combined rush was the thing to play. For a full minute they pushed the School pack towards their line, and then some rash enthusiast kicked a shade too hard. The ball dribbled out of the scrum on the School side, and Marriott punted into touch.

'You *must* let it out, you men,' said the aggrieved half-backs.

Marriott's kick had not brought much relief. The visitors were still inside the Beckford twenty-five line, and now that their forwards had realized the sin and folly of trying to rush the ball through, matters became decidedly warm for the School outsides. Norris and Gethryn in the centre and Grainger at back performed prodigies of tackling. The wing three-quarter hovered nervously about, feeling that their time might come at any moment.

The Nomad attack was concentrated on the extreme right.

Philips, the International, was officiating for them as wing-three-quarters on that side, and they played to him. If he once got the ball he would take a considerable amount of stopping. But the ball never managed to arrive. Norris and Gethryn stuck to their men closer than brothers.

A prolonged struggle on the goal-line is a great spectacle. That is why (purely in the opinion of the present scribe) Rugby is such a much better game than Association. You don't get that sort of thing in Soccer. But such struggles generally end in the same way. The Nomads were now within a couple of yards of the School line. It was a question of time. In three minutes the whistle would blow for half-time, and the School would be saved.

But in those three minutes the thing happened. For the first time in the match the Nomad forwards heeled absolutely cleanly. Hitherto, the ball had always remained long enough in the scrum to give Marriott and Wogan, the School halves, time to get round and on to their men before they could become dangerous. But this time the ball was in and out again in a moment. The Nomad half who was taking the scrum picked it up, and was over the line before Marriott realized that the ball was out at all. The school lining the ropes along the touch-line applauded politely but feebly, as was their custom when the enemy scored.

The kick was a difficult one—the man had got over in the corner—and failed. The referee blew his whistle for half-time. The teams sucked lemons, and the Beckford forwards tried to explain to Hill, the captain, why they never got that ball in the scrums. Hill having observed bitterly, as he did in every match when the School did not get thirty points in the first half, that he 'would chuck the whole lot of them out next Saturday', the game recommenced.

Beckford started on the second half with three points against them, but with both wind, what there was of it, and slope in their favour. Three points, especially in a club match, where one's opponents may reasonably be expected to suffer from lack of training and combination, is not an overwhelming score.

Beckford was hopeful and determined.

To record all the fluctuations of the game for the next thirty-five minutes is unnecessary. Copies of *The Beckfordian* containing a full report, crammed with details, and written in the most polished English, may still be had from the editor at the modest price of sixpence. Suffice it to say that two minutes from the kick-off the Nomads increased their score with a goal from a mark, and almost immediately afterwards Marriott gave the School their first score with a neat drop-kick. It was about five minutes from the end of the game, and the Nomads still led, when the event of the afternoon took place. The Nomad forwards had brought the ball down the ground with one of their combined dribbles, and a scrum had been formed on the Beckford twenty-five line. The visitors heeled as usual. The half who was taking the scrum whipped the ball out in the direction of his colleague. But before it could reach him, Wogan had intercepted the pass, and was off down the field, through the enemy's three-quarter line, with only the back in front of him, and with Norris in close attendance, followed by Gethryn.

There is nothing like an intercepted pass for adding a dramatic touch to a close game. A second before it had seemed as though the School must be beaten, for though they would probably have kept the enemy out for the few minutes that remained, they could never have worked the ball down the field by ordinary give-and-take play. And now, unless Wogan shamefully bungled what he had begun so well, victory was certain.

There was a danger, though. Wogan might in the excitement of the moment try to get past the back and score himself, instead of waiting until the back was on him and then passing to Norris. The School on the touch-line shrieked their applause, but there was a note of anxiety as well. A slight reputation which Wogan had earned for playing a selfish game sprang up before their eyes. Would he pass? Or would he run himself? If the latter, the odds were anything against his succeeding.

But everything went right. Wogan arrived at the back, drew that gentleman's undivided attention to himself, and then slung the ball out to Norris, the model of what a pass ought to be. Norris made no mistake about it.

Then the remarkable thing happened. The Bishop, having backed Norris up for fifty yards at full speed, could not stop himself at once. His impetus carried him on when all need for expenditure of energy had come to an end. He was just slowing down, leaving Norris to complete the thing alone, when to his utter amazement he found the ball in his hands. Norris had passed to him. With a clear run in, and the nearest foeman yards to the rear, Norris had passed. It was certainly weird, but his first duty was to score. There must be no mistake about the scoring. Afterwards he could do any thinking that might be required. He shot at express speed over the line, and placed the ball in the exact centre of the white line which joined the posts. Then he walked back to where Norris was waiting for him.

'Good man,' said Norris, 'that was awfully good.'

His tone was friendly. He spoke as he had been accustomed to speak before the M.C.C. match. Gethryn took his cue from him. It was evident that, for reasons at present unexplained, Norris wished for peace, and such being the case, the Bishop was only too glad to oblige him.

'No,' he said, 'it was jolly good of you to let me in like that. Why, you'd only got to walk over.'

'Oh, I don't know. I might have slipped or something. Anyhow I thought I'd better pass. What price Beckford combination? The home-made article, eh?'

'Rather,' said the Bishop.

'Oh, by the way,' said Norris, 'I was talking to young Wilson yesterday evening. Or rather he was talking to me. Decent kid, isn't he? He was telling me about Farnie. The M.C.C. match, you know, and so on.'

'Oh!' said the Bishop. He began to see how things had happened.

'Yes,' said Norris. 'Hullo, that gives us the game.'

A roar of applause from the touch-line greeted the successful attempt of Hill to convert Gethryn's try into the necessary goal. The referee performed a solo on the whistle, and immediately afterwards another, as if as an encore.

'No side,' he said pensively. The School had won by two points.

'That's all right,' said Norris. 'I say, can you come and have tea in my study when you've changed? Some of the fellows are coming. I've asked Reece and Marriott, and Pringle said he'd turn up too. It'll be rather a tight fit, but we'll manage somehow.'

'Right,' said the Bishop. 'Thanks very much.'

Norris was correct. It was a tight fit. But then a study brew loses half its charm if there is room to breathe. It was a most enjoyable ceremony in every way. After the serious part of the meal was over, and the time had arrived when it was found pleasanter to eat wafer biscuits than muffins, the Bishop obliged once more with a recital of his adventures on that distant day in the summer term.

There were several comments when he had finished. The only one worth recording is Reece's.

Reece said it distinctly reminded him of a thing which had happened to a friend of a chap his brother had known at Sandhurst.

CPSIA information can be obtained
at www.ICGtesting.com
Printed in the USA
BVHW030355040821
613604BV00007B/104

9 781978 446861